The Mardi Gras Mystery

By H. Bedford-Jones

Originally published in 1921

The Mardi Gras Mystery

Published by Resurrected Press

This classic book was handcrafted by Resurrected Press. Resurrected Press is dedicated to bringing high quality classic books back to the readers who enjoy them. These are not scanned versions of the originals, but, rather, quality checked and edited books meant to be enjoyed!

Please visit ResurrectedPress.com to view our entire catalogue!

ISBN 13: 978-1-937022-57-0

Printed in the United States of America

RESURRECTED PRESS CLASSIC MYSTERY CATALOGUE

Journeys into Mystery
Travel and Mystery in a More Elegant Time

The Edwardian Detectives
Literary Sleuths of the Edwardian Era

Gems of Mystery
Lost Jewels from a More Elegant Age

Anne Austin
One Drop of Blood
The Black Pigeon
Murder at Bridge

E. C. Bentley
Trent's Last Case: The Woman in Black

Ernest Bramah
Max Carrados Resurrected:
The Detective Stories of Max Carrados

Agatha Christie
The Secret Adversary
The Mysterious Affair at Styles

Octavus Roy Cohen
Midnight

Freeman Wills Croft
The Ponson Case
The Pit Prop Syndicate

J. S. Fletcher

The Herapath Property
The Rayner-Slade Amalgamation
The Chestermarke Instinct
The Paradise Mystery
Dead Men's Money
The Middle of Things
Ravensdene Court
Scarhaven Keep
The Orange-Yellow Diamond
The Middle Temple Murder
The Tallyrand Maxim
The Borough Treasurer
In the Mayor's Parlour
The Saftey Pin

R. Austin Freeman

The Mystery of 31 New Inn from the Dr. Thorndyke Series
John Thorndyke's Cases from the Dr. Thorndyke Series
The Red Thumb Mark from The Dr. Thorndyke Series
The Eye of Osiris from The Dr. Thorndyke Series
A Silent Witness from the Dr. John Thorndyke Series
The Cat's Eye from the Dr. John Thorndyke Series
Helen Vardon's Confession: A Dr. John Thorndyke Story
As a Thief in the Night: A Dr. John Thorndyke Story
Mr. Pottermack's Oversight: A Dr. John Thorndyke Story
Dr. Thorndyke Intervenes: A Dr. John Thorndyke Story
The Singing Bone: The Adventures of Dr. Thorndyke
The Stoneware Monkey: A Dr. John Thorndyke Story
The Great Portrait Mystery, and Other Stories: A Collection of Dr. John Thorndyke and Other Stories
The Penrose Mystery: A Dr. John Thorndyke Story
The Uttermost Farthing: A Savant's Vendetta

Arthur Griffiths
The Passenger From Calais
The Rome Express

Fergus Hume
The Mystery of a Hansom Cab
The Green Mummy
The Silent House
The Secret Passage

Edgar Jepson
The Loudwater Mystery

A. E. W. Mason
At the Villa Rose

A. A. Milne
The Red House Mystery
Baroness Emma Orczy
The Old Man in the Corner

Edgar Allan Poe
The Detective Stories of Edgar Allan Poe

Arthur J. Rees
The Hampstead Mystery
The Shrieking Pit
The Hand In The Dark
The Moon Rock
The Mystery of the Downs

Mary Roberts Rinehart
Sight Unseen and The Confession

Dorothy L. Sayers
Whose Body?

Sir William Magnay
The Hunt Ball Mystery

Mabel and Paul Thorne
The Sheridan Road Mystery

Louis Tracy
The Strange Case of Mortimer Fenley
The Albert Gate Mystery
The Bartlett Mystery
The Postmaster's Daughter
The House of Peril
The Sandling Case: What Would You Have Done?

Charles Edmonds Walk
The Paternoster Ruby

John R. Watson
The Mystery of the Downs
The Hampstead Mystery

Edgar Wallace
The Daffodil Mystery
The Crimson Circle

Carolyn Wells
Vicky Van
The Man Who Fell Through the Earth
In the Onyx Lobby
Raspberry Jam
The Clue
The Room with the Tassels
The Vanishing of Betty Varian
The Mystery Girl
The White Alley
The Curved Blades
Anybody but Anne
The Bride of a Moment

Faulkner's Folly
The Diamond Pin
The Gold Bag
The Mystery of the Sycamore
The Come Back

Raoul Whitfield
Death in a Bowl

And much more!
Visit ResurrectedPress.com
for our complete catalogue

FOREWORD

The city of New Orleans at the time of Mardi Gras would seem a natural setting for a mystery. With half the city masked and dressed in costume, no one is who they seem. And with the confusion engendered by all the parties and parades, the revelry and loss of inhibition, truly anything can happen during Carnival.

It is against this background that H. Bedford-Jones sets his novel *The Mardi Gras Mystery*. But this is not the New Orleans of today, it is the city as it was in 1921, when the culture and society of the city was still dominated by the old, established families, when Creole French was still the everyday language for many of the inhabitants, when New Orleans was still, in many ways, a world apart from the rest of the country.

But it was also a time when change was coming to the city. Prohibition had been recently enacted. And while that may not have stopped people from drinking during Mardi Gras, it did force it under cover. Other forces are also at work. Oil had recently been discovered in the bayous of Louisiana, and fueled by the new demands of the automobile a scramble was on for the mineral rights for the "black gold." Wildcat drillers and land speculators were everywhere. Fortunes were being made and lost in what had been worthless swamps just a few years earlier.

With money comes crime, some petty, some large scale and organized. Bootleggers and rum runners were becoming rampant, and the more entrepreneurial of them were seeking to broaden the scope of their activities to other areas such as gambling. And with crime comes corruption, and the insular politics of Louisiana had never had much of a reputation for honesty.

In *The Mardi Gras Mystery* Bedford-Jones ties all of these threads together into one linked package. What begins as a light-hearted tale of a gentleman-bandit soon takes a darker turn, when, as during Carnival, no one is who they seem.

It is with great pleasure that Resurrected Press offers its readers this new edition of *The Mardi Gras Mystery*, a novel by H. Bedford-Jones, "The King of the Pulps."

About the Author

Henry James O'Brien Bedford-Jones (April 29, 1887-May 6,1949) was a Canadian born author of stories and novels. After becoming an American citizen in 1908 he became a prolific writer for pulp magazines in a variety of genres including historical romances, westerns, science-fiction, and mysteries. Many of his works featured pirates. In all, he wrote over a hundred novels and earned the nickname "King of the Pulps."

Greg Fowlkes
Editor-In-Chief
Resurrected Press
www.ResurrectedPress.com

TABLE OF CONTENTS

CHAPTER 1: CARNIVAL

Jachin Fell pushed aside the glass curtains between the voluminous over-draperies in the windows of the Chess and Checkers Club, and gazed out upon the riotous streets of New Orleans. Half an hour he had been waiting here in the lounge room for Dr. Cyril Ansley, a middle-aged bachelor who had practised in Opelousas for twenty years, and who had come to the city for the Mardi Gras festivities. Another man might have seemed irritated by the wait, but Jachin Fell was quite unruffled.

He had much the air of a clerk. His features were thin and unremarkable; his pale eyes constantly wore an expression of wondering aloofness, as though he saw around him much that he vainly tried to understand. In his entire manner was a shy reticence. He was no clerk, however, this was evident from his attire. He was garbed from head to foot in soberly blending shades of gray whose richness was notable only at close view. One fancied him a very precise sort of man, an old maid of the wrong sex.

Doctor Ansley, an Inverness flung over his evening clothes, entered the lounge room, and Fell turned to him with a dry, toneless chuckle.

"You're the limit! Did you forget we were going to the Maillards' to-night?"

Ansley appeared vexed and irritated. "Confound it, Fell!" he exclaimed. "I've been all over town looking for El Reys. Caught in a crowd—no El Reys yet!"

Again Fell uttered his toneless chuckle. His voice was absolutely level, unmarked by any change of inflection.

"My dear fellow, there are only three places in the city that can afford to carry El Reys in these parlous times!

This club, however, happens to be one of the three. Here, sit down and forget your troubles over a real smoke! We need not leave for fifteen minutes yet, at least."

Doctor Ansley laid aside his cape, stick, and hat, and dropped into one of the comfortable big chairs. He accepted the proffered cigar with a sigh. Across his knees he laid an evening paper, whose flaring headlines proclaimed an extra.

"I suppose you've been gadding all around the town ever since the Revellers opened the season?" he inquired.

"Hardly," said Fell with his shy air. "I'm growing a bit stiff with age, as Eliza said when she crossed the ice. I don't gad much."

"You intend to mask for the Maillards'?" Ansley cast his eye over the gray business attire of the little man.

"I never mask." Jachin Fell shook his head. "I'll get a domino and go as I am. Excuse me—I'll order a domino now, and also provide a few more El Reys for the evening. Back in a moment."

Doctor Ansley, who was himself a non-resident member of the club and socially prominent when he could grant himself leisure for society, followed the slight figure of the other man with speculative eyes. Well as he knew Jachin Fell, he invariably found the man a source of puzzled speculation.

During many years Jachin Fell had been a member of the most exclusive New Orleans clubs. He was even received in the inner circles of Creole society, which in itself was evidence supreme as to his position. At this particular club he was famed as a wizard master of chess. He never entered a tournament, yet he consistently defeated the champions in private matches—defeated them with a bewildering ease, a shy and apologetic ease, an ease which left the beholders incredulous and aghast.

With all this, Jachin Fell was very much of a mystery, even among his closest friends. Very little was known of him; he was inconspicuous to a degree, and it was usually assumed that he was something of a recluse, the result of a thwarted love affair in his youth. He was a lawyer, and certainly maintained offices in the Maison Blanche building, but he never appeared in the courts and no case of his pleading was known.

It was said that he lived in the rebuilt casa of some old Spanish grandee in the Vieux Carre, and that this residence of his was a veritable treasure-trove of historic and beautiful things. This was mere rumour, adding a spice of romance to the general mystery. Ansley knew him as well as did most men, and Ansley knew of a few who could boast of having been a guest in Jachin Fell's home. There was a mother, an invalid of whom Fell sometimes spoke and to whom he appeared to devote himself. The family, an old one in the city, promised to die out with Jachin Fell.

Ansley puffed at his cigar and considered these things. Outside, in the New Orleans streets, was rocketing the mad mirth of carnival. The week preceding Mardi Gras was at its close. Since the beginning of the new year the festival had been celebrated in a steadily climaxing series of balls and entertainments, largely by the older families who kept to the old customs, and to a smaller extent by society at large. Now the final week was at hand, or rather the final three days—the period of the great balls, the period when tourists were flooding into town; for tourists, the whole time of Mardi Gras was comprised within these three days. Despite agonized predictions, prohibition had not adversely affected Mardi Gras or the gaiety of its celebration.

Now, as ever, was Mardi Gras symbolized by masques. In New Orleans the masquerade was not the pale and pitiful frolic of colder climes, where the occasion is but one for display of jewels and costumes, and where actual concealment of identity is a farce. Here in New Orleans were jewels and costumes in a profusion of splendour; but here was preserved the underlying idea of the masque itself—that in concealment of identity lay the life of the thing! Masquers swept the streets gaily; if harlequin husband flirted with domino wife—why, so much the merrier! There was little harm in the Latin masque, and great mirth.

When Jachin Fell returned and lighted his cigar he sank into one of the luxurious chairs beside Ansley and indicated the newspaper lying across the latter's knee, its flaring headlines standing out blackly.

"What's that about the Midnight Masquer? He's not appeared again?"

"What?" Ansley glanced at him in surprise. "You've not heard?"

Fell shook his head. "I seldom read the papers."

"Good heavens, man! He showed up last night at the Lapeyrouse dance, two minutes before midnight, as usual! A detective had been engaged, but was afterward found locked in a closet, bound with his own handcuffs. The Masquer wore his usual costume—and went through the party famously, stripping everyone in sight. Then he backed through the doors and vanished. How he got in they can't imagine; where he went they can't imagine, unless it was by airplane. He simply appeared, then vanished!"

Fell settled deeper into his chair, pointed his cigar at the ceiling, and sighed.

"Ah, most interesting! The loot was valued at about a hundred thousand?"

"I thought you said you'd not heard of it?" demanded Ansley.

Fell laughed softly and shyly. "I didn't. I merely hazarded a guess."

"Wizard!" The doctor laughed in unison. "Yes, about that amount. Exaggerated, of course; still, there were jewels of great value——"

"The Masquer is a piker," observed Fell, in his toneless voice.

"Eh? A piker—when he can make a hundred-thousand-dollar haul?"

"Don't dream that those figures represent value, Doctor. They don't! All the loot the Masquer has taken since he began work is worth little to him. Jewels are hard to sell. This game of banditry is romantic, but it's out of date these days. Of course, the crook has obtained a bit of money, but not enough to be worth the risk."

"Yet he has got quite a bit," returned Ansley, thoughtfully. "All the men have money, naturally; we don't want to find ourselves bare at some gay carnival moment! I'll warrant you've a hundred or so in your pocket right now!"

"Not I," rejoined Fell, calmly. "One ten-dollar bill. Also I left my watch at home. And I'm not dressed; I don't care to lose my pearl studs."

"Eh?" Ansley frowned. "What do you mean?"

Jachin Fell took a folded paper from his pocket and handed it to the physician.

"I met Maillard at the bank this morning. He called me into his office and handed me this—he had just received it in the mail."

Doctor Ansley opened the folded paper; an exclamation broke from him as he read the note, which was addressed to their host of the evening.

JOSEPH MAILLARD, President,
Exeter National Bank, City.

I thank you for the masque you are giving to-night. I shall be present. Please see that Mrs. M. wears her diamonds—I need them.
THE MIDNIGHT MASQUER.

Ansley glanced up. "What's this—some hoax? Some carnival jest?"

"Maillard pretended to think so." Fell shrugged his shoulders as he repocketed the note. "But he was nervous. He was afraid of being laughed at, and wouldn't go to the police. But he'll have a brace of detectives inside the house to-night, and others outside."

Ever since the first ball of the year by the Twelfth Night Club this Midnight Masquer, as he was termed, had held New Orleans gripped in terror, fascination, and vivid interest. Until a month previous to this week of Mardi Gras he had operated rarely; he had robbed with a stark and inelegant forcefulness, a brutality. Suddenly his methods changed—he appeared and transacted his business with a romantic courtesy, a daredevil gaiety; his robberies became bizarre and extraordinary.

During the past month he appeared at least once a week, now at some private ball, now at some restaurant banquet, but always in the same garb: the helmet, huge goggles and mask, and leathern clothes of a service aviator. On these occasions the throbbing roar of an airplane motor had been reported so that it was popular gossip that he landed on the roof of his designated victims and made his getaway in the same manner—by airplane. No machine had ever been seen, and the theory was believed by some, hooted at by others.

The police were helpless. The Midnight Masquer laughed openly at them and conducted his depredations with brazen unconcern, appearing where he was least expected. The anti-administration papers were clamouring about a "crime wave" and "organization of crooks," but without any visible basis for such clamours. The Midnight Masquer worked alone.

Doctor Ansley glanced at his watch, and deposited his cigar in an ash tray.

"We'd best be moving, Fell. You'll want a domino?"

"I ordered one when I got my cigars. It'll be here in a minute."

"Do you seriously think that note is genuine?"

Fell shrugged lightly. "Who knows? I'm not worried. Maillard can afford to be robbed. It will be interesting to see how he takes it if the fellow does show up."

"You're a calm one!" Ansley chuckled. "Oh, I believe the prince is to be there to-night. You've met him, I suppose?"

"No. I've had a rush of business lately, as Eliza said when she crossed the ice: haven't gone out much. Heard something about him, though. An American, isn't he? They say he's become quite popular in town."

Ansley nodded. "Quite a fine chap. His mother was an American—she married the Prince de Gramont; an international affair of the past generation. De Gramont led her a dog's life, I hear, until he was killed in a duel. She lived in Paris with the boy, sent him to school here at home, and he was at Yale when the war broke. He was technically a French subject, so he went back to serve his time.

"Still, he's an American now. Calls himself Henry Gramont, and would drop the prince stuff altogether if these French people around here would let him. He's supposed to be going into some kind of business, but just now he's having the time of his life. Every old dowager is trying to catch him."

Jachin Fell nodded. "I've no use for nobility; a rotten crowd! But this chap appears interesting. I'll be glad to size him up. Ah, here's my domino now!"

A page brought the domino. Fell, discarding the mask, threw the domino about his shoulders, and the two men left the club in company.

They sought their destination afoot—the home of the banker Joseph Maillard. The streets were riotous, filled with an eddying, laughing crowd of masquers and merrymakers of all ages and sexes; confetti twirled through the air, horns were deafening, and laughing voices rose into sharp screams of unrestrained delight.

Here and there appeared the rather constrained figures of tourists from the North. These, staid and unable to throw themselves into the utter abandon of this carnival spirit, could but stare in perplexed wonder at the scene, so alien to them, while they marvelled at the gaiety of these Southern folk who could go so far with liberty and yet not overstep the bounds of license.

At last gaining St. Charles Avenue, with the Maillard residence a half-dozen blocks distant, the two companions found themselves well away from the main carnival throngs. Even here, however, was no lack of revellers afoot for the evening—stray flotsam of the downtown crowds, or members of neighbourhood gatherings on their way to entertainment.

As the two walked along they were suddenly aware of a lithe figure approaching from the rear; with a running leap and an exclamation of delight the figure forced itself in between them, grasping an arm of either man, and a bantering voice broke in upon their train of talk.

"Forfeit!" it cried. "Forfeit—where are your masks, sober gentlemen? This grave physician may be pardoned, but not a domino who refuses to mask! And for forfeit you shall be my escort and take me whither you are going."

Laughing, the two fell into step, glancing at the gay figure between them. A Columbine, she was both cloaked and masked. Encircling her hair was a magnificent scarf shot with metal designs of solid gold—a most unusual thing. Also, from her words it was evident that she had recognized them.

"Willingly, fair Columbine," responded Fell in his dry and unimpassioned tone of voice. "We shall be most happy, indeed, to protect and take you with us——"

"So far as the door, at least," interrupted Ansley, with evident caution. But Fell drily laughed aside this wary limitation.

"Nay, good physician, farther!" went on Fell. "Our Columbine has an excellent passport, I assure you. This gauzy scarf about her raven tresses was woven for the good Queen Hortense, and I would venture a random guess that, clasped about her slender throat, lies the queen's collar of star sapphires——"

"Oh!" From the Columbine broke a cry of warning and swift dismay. "Don't you dare speak my name, sir—don't you dare!"

Fell assented with a chuckle, and subsided.

Ansley regarded his two companions with sidelong curiosity. He could not recognize Columbine, and he could not tell whether Fell were speaking of the scarf and jewels in jest or earnest. Such historic things were not uncommon in New Orleans, yet Ansley never heard of these particular treasures. However, it seemed that Fell knew their companion, and accepted her as a fellow guest at the Maillard house.

"What are you doing out on the streets alone?" demanded Fell, suddenly. "Haven't you any friends or relatives to take care of you?"

Columbine's laughter pealed out, and she pressed Fell's arm confidingly.

"Have I not some little rights in the world, monsieur?" she said in French. "I have been mingling with the dear crowds and enjoying them, before I go to be buried in the dull splendours of the rich man's house. Tell me, do you think that the Midnight Masquer will make an appearance to-night?"

"I have every reason to believe that he will," said Jachin Fell, gravely.

Columbine put one hand to her throat, and shivered a trifle.

"You—you really think so? You are not trying to frighten me?" Her voice was no longer gay. "But—the jewels——"

"Wear them, wear them!" There was command in the tone of Fell. "Were they not given you to wear to-night? Then wear them, by all means. Don't worry, my dear."

Columbine said nothing for a moment; her gaiety seemed to be suddenly extinguished and quenched. Ansley was wondering uneasily at the constraint, when at length she broke the silence.

"Since you have ordered, let the command be obeyed!" She essayed a laugh, which appeared rather forced. "Yet, if they are lost and are taken by the Masquer——"

"In that case," said Fell, "let the blame be mine entirely. If they are lost, little Columbine, others will be lost with them, fear not! I think that this party would be a rich haul for the Masquer, eh? Take the rich man and his friends—they could bear plucking, that crowd! Rogues all."

"Confound you, Fell!" exclaimed Ansley, uneasily. "If the bandit does show up there would be the very devil to pay!"

"And Maillard would do the paying." Fell's dry chuckle held a note of bitterness. "Let him. Who cares? Look at his house, there, blazing with lights. Who pays for those lights? The people his financial tentacles have closed their sucker-like grip upon. His wife's jewels have been purchased with the coin of oppression and injustice. His son's life is one of roguery and drunken wildness——"

"Man, are you mad?" Ansley indicated the Columbine between them. "We're not alone here—you must not talk that way——"

Jachin Fell only chuckled again. Columbine's laugh broke in with renewed gaiety:

"Nonsense, my dear Galen! We surely may be allowed to be ourselves during carnival! Away with the heresies of hypocritical society. Our friend speaks the sober truth. We masquers may admit among ourselves that Bob Maillard is——"

"Is not the man we would have our daughters marry, provided we had daughters," said Fell. Then he gestured toward the house ahead of them, and his tone changed: "Still, now that we are about to enter that house, we must remind ourselves of courtesy and the limitations of guests. Say no more. Produce your invitation, Columbine, for I think we shall find that the doors to-night are guarded by Cerberus."

They had come to a file of limousines and cars, and approached the gateway of the Maillard home. They turned into the gate.

The house loomed before them, a great house set amid gardens, stately in the fashion of olden days. The lower floors were discreetly darkened to the streets, but on the upper floor, where was the ballroom with its floor of cypress, there was a glitter of bright lights and open windows. Music drifted to them as they approached. Jachin Fell touched the arm of Ansley and indicated an inconspicuous figure to one side of the entrance steps.

"An outer guardian," he murmured. "Our host, it seems, is neglecting no precaution! I feel sorry for the Masquer, if he appears here."

They came to the doorway. Columbine produced an invitation, duly numbered, and the three entered the house together.

CHAPTER 2: MASQUERS

Joseph Maillard might have hopefully considered the note from the Midnight Masquer to be a hoax perpetrated by some of his friends, but he took no chances. Two detectives were posted in the grounds outside the house; inside, two others, masked and costumed, were keeping a quietly efficient eye on all that transpired.

Each guest upon entering was conducted directly to the presence of Joseph Maillard himself, or of his wife; was bidden to unmask in this private audience, and was then presented with a favour and sent forth masked anew to the festivities. These favours were concealed, in the case of the ladies, in corsage bouquets; in that of the men, inside false cigars. There was to be a general opening of the favours at midnight, the time set for unmasking. All this ceremony was regarded by the guests as a delightful innovation, and by Joseph Maillard as a delightful way of assuring himself that only the invited guests entered his house. Invitations might be forged—faces, never!

Lucie Ledanois entered the presence of her stately relative, and after unmasking, dutifully exchanged kisses with Mrs. Maillard. Until some months previously, until she had come into the management of her own property—or what was left of it—Lucie had been the ward of the Maillards. Their former attitude of possession still lingered, but they were relatives for whom she felt little real affection.

"Mercy, child, how marvellous you look to-night!" exclaimed Mrs. Maillard, holding her off and examining her high colour with obvious suspicion. Mrs. Maillard was herself rather plump and red, and stern of eye into the bargain. She was a keen, masterful woman.

"Thank you, ma'am," and Lucie made a mock courtesy. "Do you like little Columbine?"

"Very much. Here's Aunt Sally; take Miss Lucie's cloak, Sally."

An old coloured servant bobbed her head in greeting to Lucie, who removed her cloak. As she did so, she saw that Mrs. Maillard's voice died away, and that the lady's eyes were fastened in utter amazement upon her throat.

"Isn't it pretty, auntie?" she asked, smilingly. This was straining the relationship a trifle, but it was a custom which Lucie usually followed with the family.

"My goodness gracious!" The stern eyes hardened. "Where—where on earth did *you* obtain such a thing? Why—why——"

Columbine's features flinched. She was a poor relation, of course, so the look in the older woman's eyes and the implication of the words formed little less than an insult.

Quietly she put one hand to her throat and removed the collar, dropping it into the hand of Mrs. Maillard. It was a thing to make any woman's eyes widen—a collar of exquisitely wrought gold studded with ten great blazing star sapphires. Beside it the diamonds that bejewelled Mrs. Maillard's ample front looked cold and lifeless.

"That?" queried Lucie, innocently, producing a scrap of chamois and dabbing at her nose. "Oh, that's very interesting! It was made for Queen Hortense—so was this scarf that keeps my ragged hair from lopping out!"

"You didn't buy them, certainly!" demanded Mrs. Maillard.

"Of course not. They were a present—only this morning."

"Girl!" The lady's voice was harsh. "A present? From whom, if you please?"

"Oh, I promised not to tell; he's a particular friend of mine. Aren't the stones pretty?"

Mrs. Maillard was speechless. She compressed her firm lips and watched Lucie replace the sapphire collar without a word to offer. Silently she extended a corsage bouquet from the pile beside her; then, in a trembling voice, forced herself to explain about the favour inside.

"And I hope," she added, "that before receiving any more such valuable presents you'll consult *me*. Of course, if you don't wish to tell about this, you needn't; but a word of advice will often save a girl from making very serious mistakes."

"Thank you, auntie dear," and Lucie nodded as she pinned the bouquet. "You're just as dear to me as you can be! See you later."

Slipping her mask into place she was gone, not without relief. She knew very well that within half an hour Bob Maillard would be informed that she had accepted gifts of jewels from other men, with all the accompanying implications and additions that imagination could furnish. For, although Bob Maillard wanted very much indeed to marry her his mother had no intention of sanctioning such a union.

"Neither has Uncle Joseph," she reflected, smiling to herself, "and neither have I! So we're all agreed, except Bob."

"Columbine!" A hand fell upon her wrist. "Columbine! Turn and confess thy sins!"

A cry of instinctive alarm broke from the girl; she turned, only to break into a laugh of chagrin at her own fright.

She had come to the foot of the wide, old-fashioned stairway that led to the floors above, and beside her had suddenly appeared a Franciscan monk, cowled and gowned in sober brown from head to foot.

"You frightened me, holy man!" she cried, gaily. "Confess to you, indeed! Not I."

"Never a better chance, butterfly of the world!" It was a voice that she dimly recognized, yet she could not name the owner: a merry, carefree voice that was slightly disguised.

"Never a better chance," and the Franciscan offered his arm. "Haste not to the dance, fair sister—tarry a while and invite the soul in speech of import! Having passed the dragon at the gate, tarry a moment with this man of vows——"

"Shrive me quickly, then," she said, laughing.

"Now, without confession? Would you have me read your thoughts and give penance?"

"If you can do that, holy man, I may confess; so prove it quickly!"

For the moment they stood alone. Higher on the stairs, and among the rooms behind them, were gay groups of masquers—dominoes, imposing Mephistos, backwoodsmen, gallants of Spain and France, red Indians and turbaned Hindus.

The Franciscan leaned forward. His voice came low, distinct, clear-cut, and he spoke in the French which Lucie understood as another mother-tongue, as do most of the older families of New Orleans.

"See how I read them, mademoiselle! One thought is of uneasy suspicion; it is typified by a hard-lipped, grasping man. One thought is of profound regret; it is typified by a darkly welling stream of oil. One thought——"

Suddenly Lucie had shrunk away from him. "Who— who are you?" she breathed, with a gasp that was almost of fear. "Who are you, monsieur?"

"A humble brother of minor orders," and he bowed. "Shall I not continue with my reading? The third thought, mademoiselle, is one of hope; it is typified by a small man who is dressed all in gray——"

Lucie turned away from him quickly.

"I think that you have made some grave error, monsieur," she said. Her voice was cold, charged with dismissal and offended dignity. "I pray you, excuse me."

Not waiting any response, she hastily ran up the stairs. After her, for a moment, gazed the Franciscan, then shrugged his wide shoulders and plunged into the crowd.

The ballroom on the top floor was throbbing with music, gay with costumes and decorations, thronged with dancing couples. Into the whirl of it pirouetted Columbine. Almost at once she found herself dancing with a gorgeously attired Musketeer; she separated from him as quickly as possible, for she recognized him as Bob Maillard. Nor did he find her again, although he searched, not knowing her identity; for she evaded him.

While she danced, while she chattered and laughed and entered into the mad gaiety of the evening, Lucie Ledanois could not banish from her mind that ominous Franciscan. How could he have known? How could he have guessed what only she and one other barely suspected? There was no proof, of course; the very breath of suspicion seemed a calumny against an upright man!

Joseph Maillard had sold that Terrebonne land six months before any gas or oil had been discovered there, and eight months before Lucie had come into the management of her own affairs. He had not known about the minerals, of course; it was a case only of bad judgment. Yet, indubitably, he was now a shareholder and officer in the Bayou Oil Company, the concern which had bought that strip of land.

Two years previously Maillard had sold that swamp land up in St. Landry parish; the land had been drained and sectioned off by real estate people at enormous profit.

Lucie strove angrily to banish the dark thoughts from her mind. Why, Maillard was a rich man, a banker, an honorable gentleman! To doubt his honour, although he was a harsh and a stern man, was impossible. Lucie knew him better than most, and could not believe——

"May I crave pardon for my error?" came a voice at her elbow. She turned, to see the Franciscan again beside her. "With a thousand apologies for impertinence, mademoiselle; I am very sorry for my faults. Will not that admission obtain for me one little dance, one hint of forgiveness from fair Columbine?"

Something in his voice spelt sincerity. Lucie, smiling, held out her hand.

"You are pardoned, holy man. If you can dance in that friar's robe, then try it!"

Could he dance, indeed! Who could not dance with Columbine for partner? So saying, the monk proved his word by the deed and proved it well. Nor did he again hint that he had recognized her; until, as they parted, he once more left her astonished and perturbed. As he bowed he murmured:

"Beware, sweet Columbine! Beware of the gay Aramis! Beware of his proposals!"

He was gone upon the word.

Aramis? Why, that must be the Musketeer, of course—Bob Maillard! The name, with its implications, was a clever hit. But who was this brown monk, who seemed to know so much, who danced so divinely, whose French was like music? A vague suspicion was in the girl's mind, but she had no proof.

Half an hour after this Bob Maillard came to her, and with impatient words made a path through the circle which surrounded her. He caught her hand and bent over it with an affectation of gallantry which became him well, for in his costume he made a handsome figure.

"I know you now, Lucie!" he murmured. "I must see you at once—in the conservatory."

She was minded to refuse, but assented briefly. The words of the monk intrigued her; what had the man guessed? If Bob were indeed about to propose, she would this time cut off his hopes for good. But—was it that sort of a proposal?

As she managed to rid herself of her admirers, and descended to the conservatory, she was highly vexed with herself and the Franciscan, and so came to her appointment in no equable frame of mind. She found Maillard waiting in the old-fashioned conservatory; he had unmasked, and was puffing a cigarette. His heavy features and bold, shrewd eyes were fastened hungrily upon her as he came to meet her.

"By gad, Lucie, you're beautiful to-night!"

"Thanks, cousin Robert. Was it for that——?"

"No! See here, where did you get that collar of jewels?"

"Indeed!" The girl proudly drew herself up. "What business is that of yours, sir?"

"Aren't you one of the family? It's our business to protect your rep——"

"Be careful!" Anger trembled in her voice, cut off his words. "Be careful!"

"But damn it—Lucie! Don't you know that I want to marry you——"

"My dear Robert, I certainly do not want to marry any man who swears to my face—you least of all!" she coldly intervened. "I have already refused you three times; let this be the fourth and last. I owe you no account of my possessions nor where I get them; I am entirely capable of managing my own affairs. Now, kindly inform me why you wished me to meet you here. Also, you know that I don't like cigarette smoke."

Sulkily, Maillard threw away his cigarette; with an effort he calmed himself. He was anything but a fool, this young man. He was rather clever, and saw that he had so long considered his pretty cousin a personal possession that he was now in some danger of losing her.

"I have a chance to make some money for you in a hurry," he said. "Your father left you a good deal of land up Bayou Terrebonne way——"

"Your father sold some of it," she put in, idly. His eyes flickered to the thrust.

"Yes; but you've plenty left, near Paradis. It's away from the gas field, but I'm interested in an oil company. We've plenty of money, and we're going to go strong after the liquid gold. That land of yours is good for nothing else, and if you want to make some money out of it I'll swing the company into leasing at a good figure and drilling there."

"You think there's oil on the land?"

"No." He made a swift, energetic gesture of dissent. "To be frank, I don't. But I'd like to throw a bit of luck your way, Lucie. We're getting a lot of money into the company, and some brains. That fellow Gramont—the prince, you know him—he's an engineer and a geologist, and he's in the swim."

"So," the girl smiled a little, "you would betray your business friends in order to make a bit of money for me?"

Maillard stared at her. "Well, if you put it that way, yes! I'd do more than that for——"

"Thank you," she interrupted, her voice cold. "I don't think I'd trust your sagacity very far, Robert. Good-night."

She turned from him and was gone, dancing through the great rooms like a true Columbine. Later he saw her among the dancers above, although he obtained no further speech with her.

Midnight neared, and brought a concern to many; the Midnight Masquer had gained his name by invariably appearing a moment or two before the stroke of twelve. Jachin Fell, who divided his time between enjoying the smoking room and wandering about among the masquers, perceived that Joseph Maillard was watching the time with anxiety.

A large man, stern and a bit scornful of look, Maillard was imposing rather than handsome. He appeared the typical banker, efficient, devoid of all sentiment. Amused by the man's evident uneasiness, Jachin Fell kept him in view while the moments dragged. One might have thought that the little gray man was studying the financier as an entomologist studies a butterfly on a pin.

Shortly before twelve Columbine pirouetted up to Jachin Fell and accepted the arm he offered her. They were for the moment alone, in a corner of the ballroom.

"I must see you to-morrow, please," she breathed.

"Gladly," he assented. "May I call? It's Sunday, you know——"

"If you will; at three. Something has happened, but I cannot speak of it here. Does any one else know that you—that you are interested in my affairs?"

The pale gray eyes of the little gray man looked very innocent and wondering.

"Certainly not, my dear! Why?"

"I'll tell you to-morrow." Then she broke into a laugh. "Well, it is midnight—and the Masquer has not appeared! I'm almost sorry."

The lights flickered off for a moment, then on again. The signal for unmasking!

The dancing ceased. From the whole room arose a babel of voices—cries of surprise, exclamations, merry laughter. Columbine removed her mask. An instant later Joseph Maillard approached them, chuckling to himself and looking hugely relieved.

"Ha, Lucie! I guessed you beneath the Columbine daintiness! Well, Jachin, it was a hoax after all, eh? Some confounded joke. Come down to the library in five minutes, will you? A meeting of the select circle, to discuss prohibition."

"Aren't you going to invite me, Uncle Joseph?" broke in Lucie, gaily.

"No, no, little one!" Maillard reproved her, laughingly. "Look not upon the silver cup at your age, my dear. Have you examined your favour yet?"

Remembering, the girl caught at her corsage. Cries of delight were arising on all sides as the favours were revealed—most handsome favours, even for Mardi Gras! From the heart of the rosebuds in her hand Lucie removed a brooch of old filigree work set with a group of pearls. She glanced about for Jachin Fell, but he had vanished with Maillard. A voice rose at her elbow:

"Mademoiselle, you are not less lucky than beautiful! Pearls to the pearl!"

She turned to see the Franciscan—no longer masked, but now gazing at her from a frank, laughing countenance, still partially veiled by the brown cowl that was drawn up close about his head.

"Henry Gramont!" she exclaimed. "Oh, I half suspected that it was you——"

"But you were not sure?" he chuckled. "You're not offended with me, Lucie?"

"I should be." She tossed her head. "You were impertinent, M. le prince!"

He made a distasteful gesture. "None of that, Lucie! You know I don't like it——"

"Oh, la, la!" she mocked him. "M. le prince is seeing America, *n'est ce pas*? He has come to America to find a rich wife, is it not?"

Gramont's face lost its smile, and suddenly became almost harsh.

"I shall call upon you at four to-morrow, Lucie," he said, abruptly, and turned. Nor did he pause to get her reply. An instant afterward Lucie was surrounded by a merry group of friends, and she saw no more of Henry Gramont.

About five minutes later those in the ballroom distinctly heard, through the open windows, the heavy pulsations of an airplane motor.

Chapter 3: The Bandit

Joseph Maillard's library was on the ground floor of the house; it was a sedate and stately room, and was invariably shut off to itself. Not even to-night, of all nights, was it thrown open with the remainder of the house.

Here, for a good half hour, had been Uncle Neb. The old butler was mysteriously engaged with certain tall silver goblets, fragrant mint, and yet more fragrant—if illegal—bottles. And it was here that Joseph Maillard summoned half a dozen of his particular cronies and friends, after the stroke of midnight had assured him that there was no danger to be expected from the bandit. His son was not among the number. The half dozen were nearly all elderly men, and, with the exception of Jachin Fell, all were men of prominent affairs.

About the table grouped Maillard and his guests, while in the background hovered Uncle Neb, glistening black, hugely important, and grinning widely. Fell was the last to enter the room, and as he did so old Judge Forester turned to him smilingly.

"Ah, here is an attorney in whom there is no guile! Jachin, come and settle a dispute. I maintain that the dignity of the law is not less now than in the old days; that it has merely accommodated itself to changing conditions, and that it is a profession for gentlemen now as always. Jules, state your argument!"

Jules Delagroux, a white-haired Creole lawyer of high standing, smiled a trifle sadly.

"My case," he said, "is that the old days are dead; that the law is no longer a profession, but a following for charlatans. In a word, that the law has been killed by the lawyers." He gestured finality and glanced at Fell.

"So?" Jachin Fell smiled in his shy fashion. "Gentlemen, I heartily agree with you both. I am an attorney, but I do not practise because I cannot accommodate myself to those very changing conditions of which Judge Forester speaks. To-day, the lawyer must be a politician; he must be an adept in the trick of words and deeds; he must be able not to serve his profession but to make it serve him, and he must remember always that the rights of property are more sacred than those of life and liberty. Otherwise, he will remain honest and poor."

An ejaculation of "True" from the judge brought smiles. Jachin Fell continued whimsically:

"Regarding these very conditions many years ago, gentlemen, I was tempted to change my profession—but to what? I was tempted to enter the church until I saw that the same conditions hold good of a clergyman. I was tempted to enter medicine until I saw that they also held true of a doctor. I was tempted to other things, always with the like result. Well, you know the story of Aunt Dixie and her black underwear—'Honey, I ain't ashamed of mah grief; when I mourns, I *mourns*!' Even so with the law——"

A burst of laughter drowned him out, and the original argument was forgotten. Maillard, standing before a small wall safe that flanked the open hearth, lifted his silver goblet, asteam with beads. The moment for which he had been waiting was here; he launched his little thunderbolt with an air of satisfied importance.

"My friends, I have a confession to make!" he announced. "To-day I received a note from the Midnight Masquer stating that he would be with us this evening, presumably at the hour of midnight, his usual time."

These words brought an instant silence. Uncle Neb, from his corner, uttered a startled "Fore de lawd!" that rang through the room; yet no one smiled. The half-dozen men were tense, watchful, astonished. But Maillard swung up his silver cup and laughed gaily.

"I took full precautions, gentlemen. The hour of danger is past, and the notorious bandit has not arrived— or, if he has arrived, he is now in the hands of the law. After all, that note may have been something in the nature of a carnival jest! So up with your cups, my friends—a lifelong health to Mardi Gras, and damnation to prohibition and the Midnight Masquer!"

From everyone broke a swift assent to the toast, a murmur of relieved tension. The silver goblets were lifted, touched in a musical clinking of edges, and the aromatic breath of juleps filled the library as the drinkers, in true Southern fashion, buried noses in the fragrant mint. Then, as the cups were lowered, from the recess of the curtained windows at one end of the room came a quiet voice:

"I thank you, gentlemen! But I must remind you, Maillard, that there was not a time limit set in the note."

With a simultaneous gasp everyone turned. Maillard staggered; his face went livid. Uncle Neb, who had been advancing to refill the cups, dropped his silver tray with a crash that went unheeded, indeed unheard. Every eye was fastened upon that amazing figure now advancing from the shadows of the recess.

It was the figure of an aviator, clad in leather from top to toe, the goggles and helmet shield completely masking his head and features from recognition. In his hand he held an automatic pistol, which covered the group of men before him with its threatening mouth.

"Not a sound, if you please," he warned, his voice thin and nasal—obviously disguised. "I trust that none of you gentlemen is armed, because I am very quick on the trigger. A very pleasant surprise, Maillard? You'd given me up, eh?"

For an instant no one spoke. Then Maillard moved slightly, moved his hand toward a button set in the wall near the safe. The voice of the bandit leaped out at him like thin steel:

"Quiet, you fool! If you touch that button——"

Maillard stiffened, and gripped the table edge with his shaking hand.

"This is an outrage, suh!" began Judge Forester, his white goatee bristling. The bandit bowed slightly, and addressed the gathering in a tone of dry raillery:

"An outrage? Exactly. You were just now discussing the majesty of the law. Well, I assure you that I found your discussion intensely interesting. Mr. Fell correctly stated that the rights of property are more sacred in legal eyes than the rights of human life. You see, gentlemen, the discussion touched me very closely!

"I am now engaged in outraging the law, and I have this amendment to propose to Mr. Fell: That if he had been tempted to follow the profession of a robber he would have found the same conditions prevailing which he quoted as applying to other professions."

Jachin Fell, alone of those about the table, allowed a smile to curve his lips.

"The rights of property," pursued the bandit with a deadly smoothness, "are to me, also, far more sacred than human life; there I agree with the law. So, gentlemen, kindly empty your pockets on the table." His voice became crisp. "The jewelled scarf-pins which you received as favours this evening may be added to the collection; otherwise, I shall not touch your private possessions. No watches, thank you. Maillard, kindly begin! I believe that you carry a wallet? If you please."

The banker could not but obey. His hands trembling with fear and rage, he took from his pocket a wallet, and emptied a sheaf of bills upon the table. One after another, the other men followed his example. The bandit made no attempt to search them, but watched with eyes that glittered from behind his mask as they laid money and scarf-pins on the table. When it came his turn, Jachin Fell drew a single bill from his pocket, and laid it down.

"You put some faith in that warning, Mr. Fell?" The bandit laughed. "Do you think that you will know me again?"

"I hardly believe so, sir," answered Fell in his apologetic fashion. "Your disguise is really excellent."

"Thank you." The bandit's voice held a thin mockery. "Coming from you, sir, that compliment is most welcome."

"What the devil does the fellow mean?" exploded Judge Forester.

"Then you are not aware that Mr. Fell is a man of large affairs?" The bandit's white teeth flashed in a smile. "He is a modest man, this attorney! And a dangerous man also, I assure you. But come, Mr. Fell, I'll not betray you."

Jachin Fell obviously did not appreciate the pleasantry. His shy and wondering features assumed a set and hardened look.

"Whoever you are," he responded, a subtle click of anger in his tone, "you shall be punished for this!"

"For what, Mr. Fell? For knowing too much of your private affairs?" The bandit laughed. "Fear not—I am only an amateur at this game, fortunately! So do your worst, and my blessing upon you! Now, gentlemen, kindly withdraw a few paces and join Uncle Neb yonder against the wall. All but you, Maillard; I'm not through with you yet."

The automatic pistol gestured; under its menace everyone obeyed the command, for the calm assurance of the bandit made it seem extremely likely that he would use the weapon without compunction. The men withdrew toward the far end of the room, where a word from the aviator halted them. Maillard remained standing where he was, his heavy features now mottled with impotent anger.

The Masquer advanced to the table and gathered the heap of money and scarfpins into the leathern pocket of his coat. During the process his gaze did not waver from the group of men, nor did the threat of his weapon lift from the banker before him.

"Now, Maillard," he quietly ordered, "you will have the kindness to turn around and open the wall safe behind you. And don't touch the button."

Maillard started.

"That safe! Why—why—damn you, I'll do nothing of the sort!"

"If you don't," was the cool threat, "I'll shoot you through the abdomen. A man fears a bullet there worse than death. It may kill you, and it may not; really, I care very little. You—you financier!"

Scorn leaped into the quiet voice, scorn that lashed and bit deep.

"You money trickster! Do you think I would spare such a man as you? You draw your rents from the poor and destitute, your mortgages cover half the parishes in the state, and in your heart is neither compassion nor pity for man or woman. You take the property of others from behind the safety curtain of the law; I do it from behind a pistol! I rob only those who can afford to lose— am I really as bad as you, in the eyes of morality and ethics? Bah! I could shoot you down without a qualm!"

In his voice was so deadly a menace that Maillard trembled. Yet the banker drew himself up and struggled for self-control, stung as he was by this flood of vituperation before the group of his closest friends.

"There is nothing of mine in that safe," he said, his voice a low growl. "I have given it to my son to use. He is not here."

"That," said the Masquer, calmly, "is exactly why I desire you to open it. Your son must make his contribution, for I keenly regret his absence. If you are a criminal, he is worse! You rob and steal under shelter of the law, but you have certain limitations, certain bounds of an almost outgrown honour. He has none, that son of yours. Why, he would not hesitate to turn your own tricks back upon you, to rob *you*, if he could! Open that safe or take the consequences; no more talk, now!"

The command cracked out like a whiplash. With a shrug of helplessness the banker turned and fumbled with the protruding knob of the safe. With one exception all eyes were fastened upon this amazing Masquer. The exception was Jachin Fell, who, suddenly alert and watchful, had turned his attention to Maillard and the safe, a keen speculation in his gaze as though he were wondering what that steel vault would produce.

All were silent. There was something about this Midnight Masquer that held them intently. Perhaps some were inclined to think him a jester, one of the party masquerading under the famous bandit's guise; if so, his last words to Maillard had removed all such thought. That indictment had been deadly and terrible—and true, as they knew. Bob Maillard was not greatly admired by those among his father's friends who best knew him.

Now the door of the safe swung open. The compartments appeared empty.

"Take out the drawers and turn them up over the table," commanded the Masquer.

Maillard obeyed. He took several of the small drawers, and all proved to be empty; this development drew a dry chuckle from Jachin Fell. Then, from the last drawer, there fell out on the table a large envelope, sealed. The Masquer leaned forward, seized upon this envelope, and crushed it into his pocket.

"Thank you," he observed. "That is all."

"Damn you!" cried Maillard, shaking a fist. "You'd try blackmail, would you?"

The bandit regarded him a moment, then laughed.

"If you knew what was in that envelope, my dear financier, you might not speak so hastily. If I knew what was in it, I might answer you. But I don't know. I only suspect—and hope."

While he spoke the bandit was backing toward the door that opened upon the lower hallway of the house. He drew this door open, glanced swiftly out into the hall, and then placed the key on the outside.

"And now, my friends—*au revoir!*"

The Masquer sprang backward into the hall. The door slammed, the key clicked. He was gone!

Maillard was the first to wake into voice and action. "The other door!" he cried. "Into the dining room——"

He flung open a second door and dashed into the dining room, followed by the other men. Here the windows, giving upon the garden, were open. Then Maillard came to a sudden halt, and after him the others; through the night was pulsating, with great distinctness, the throbbing roar of an airplane motor! From Maillard broke a bitter cry:

"The detectives—I'll get the fools here! You gentlemen search the house; Uncle Neb, go with them, into every room! That fellow can't possibly have escaped——"

"No word of alarm to the ladies," exclaimed Judge Forester, hurriedly. "If he was not upstairs, then they have seen nothing of him. We must divide and search."

They hastily separated. Maillard dashed away to summon the detectives, also to get other men to aid in the search.

The result was vain. Within twenty minutes the entire house, from cellar to garret, had been thoroughly gone over, without causing any alarm to the dancers in the ballroom. Maillard began to think himself a little mad. No one had been seen to enter or leave the house, and certainly there had been no airplane about. The Masquer had not appeared except in the library, and now he was most indubitably not in the house. By all testimony, he had neither entered it nor left it!

"Well, I'm damned!" said Maillard, helplessly, to Judge Forester, when the search was concluded. "Not a trace of the scoundrel! Here, Fell—can't you help us out? Haven't you discovered a thing?"

"Nothing," responded Jachin Fell, calmly.

At this instant Bob Maillard rushed up. He had just learned of the Masquer's visit. In response to his excited questioning his father described the scene in the library and added:

"I trust there was nothing important among those papers of yours, Robert?"

"No," said the younger man. "No. Nothing valuable at all."

Henry Gramont was passing. He caught the words and paused, his gaze resting for an instant upon the group. A faint smile rested upon his rather harshly drawn features.

"I just found this," he announced, holding out a paper. "It was pinned to the outside of the library door. I presume that your late visitor left it as a memento?"

Jachin Fell took the paper, the other men crowding around him.

"Ah, Maillard! The same handwriting as that of your letter!"

Upon the paper was pencilled a single hasty line:

My compliments to Robert Maillard—and my thanks.

Bob Maillard sprang forward, angrily inspecting the paper. When he relinquished it, Fell calmly claimed it again.

"Confound the rogue!" muttered the banker's son, turning away. His features were pale, perhaps with anger. "There was nothing but stock certificates in that envelope—and they can be reissued."

The festivities were not broken up. As much could hardly be said for the host, who felt keenly the verbal lashing that had been administered to him before his friends. News of the robbery gradually leaked out among the guests; the generally accepted verdict was that the Masquer had appeared, only to be frightened away before he could secure any loot.

It was nearly two in the morning when Jachin Fell, who was leaving, encountered Henry Gramont at the head of the wide stairway. He halted and turned to the younger man.

"Ah—have you a pencil, if you please?"

"I think so, Mr. Fell." Gramont felt beneath his Franciscan's robe, and extended a pencil.

Jachin Fell examined it, brought a paper from beneath his domino, and wrote down a word. The paper was that on which the farewell message of the Midnight Masquer had been written.

"A hard lead, a very hard point indeed!" said Fell. He pocketed the paper again and regarded Gramont steadily as he returned the pencil. "Few men carry so hard a pencil, sir."

"You're quite right," and Gramont smiled. "I borrowed this from Bob Maillard only a moment ago. Its hardness surprised me."

"Oh!" said Jachin Fell, mildly. "By the way, aren't you the Prince de Gramont? When we met this evening, you were introduced as plain Mr. Gramont, but it seems to me that I had heard something——"

"Quite a mistake, Mr. Fell. I'm no prince; simply Henry Gramont, and nothing more. Also, an American citizen. Some of these New Orleans people can't forget the prince business, most unfortunately."

"Ah, yes," agreed Fell, shyly. "Do you know, a most curious thing——"

"Yes?" prompted Gramont, his eyes intent upon the little gray man.

"That paper you brought us—the paper which you found pinned to the library door," said Fell, apologetically. "Do you know, Mr. Gramont, that oddly enough there were no pin holes in that paper?"

Gramont smiled faintly, as though he were inwardly amused over the remark.

"Not at all curious," he said, his voice level. "It was pinned rather stoutly—I tore off the portion bearing the message. I'll wager that you'll find the end of the paper still on the door downstairs. You might make certain that its torn edge fits that of the paper in your pocket; if it did not, then the fact *would* be curious! I am most happy to have met you, Mr. Fell. I trust that we shall meet again, often."

With a smile, he extended his hand, which Mr. Fell shook cordially.

As Jachin Fell descended the wide staircase his face was red—quite red. One would have said that he had just been worsted in some encounter, and that the sense of defeat still rankled within him.

Upon gaining the lower hall he glanced at the door of the library. There, still pinned to the wood where it had been unregarded by the passersby, was a small scrap of paper. Mr. Fell glanced at it again, then shook his head and slowly turned away, as though resisting a temptation.

"No," he muttered. "No. It would be sure to fit the paper in my pocket. It would be sure to fit, confound him!"

A little later he left the house and walked along the line of cars that were waiting parked in the drive and in the street outside. Before one of the cars he came to a halt, examining it closely. The sleepy chauffeur got out and touched his cap in a military salute; he was a sturdy young fellow, his face very square and blunt.

"A very handsome car. May I ask whose it is?" inquired Fell, mildly.

"Mr. Gramont's, sir," answered the chauffeur.

"Ah, thank you. A very handsome car indeed. Good-night!"

Mr. Fell walked away, striding briskly down the avenue. When he approached the first street light he came to a pause, and began softly to pat his person as though searching for something.

"I told you that you'd pay for knowing too much about me, young man!" he said, softly. "What's this, now—what's this?"

A slight rustle of paper, as he walked along, had attracted his attention. He passed his hands over the loose, open domino that cloaked him; he detected a scrap of paper pinned to it in the rear. He loosened the paper, and under the street light managed to decipher the writing which it bore.

A faint smile crept to his lips as he read the pencilled words:

I do not love you, Jachin Fell,

The reason why I cannot tell; But this I know, and know full well, I do not love you, Jachin Fell!

"Certainly the fellow has wit, if not originality," muttered Mr. Fell, as he carefully stowed away the paper. The writing upon it was in the hand of the Midnight Masquer.

CHAPTER 4: CALLERS

The house in which Lucie Ledanois lived had been her mother's; the furniture and other things in it had been her mother's; the two negro servants, who spoke only the Creole French patois, had been her mother's. It was a small house, but very beautiful inside. The exterior betrayed a lack of paint or the money with which to have painting done.

The Ledanois family, although distantly connected with others such as the Maillards, had sent forth its final bud of fruition in the girl Lucie. Her mother had died while she was yet an infant, and through the years she had companioned her father, an invalid during the latter days. He had never been a man to count dollars or costs, and to a large extent he had outworn himself and the family fortunes in a vain search for health.

With Lucie he had been in Europe at the outbreak of war, and had come home to America only to die shortly afterward. Once deprived of his fine recklessness, the girl had found her affairs in a bad tangle. Under the guardianship of Maillard the tangle had been somewhat resolved and simplified, but even Maillard would appear to have made mistakes, and of late Lucie had against her will suspected something amiss in the matter of these mistakes.

It was natural, then, that she should take Jachin Fell into her confidence. Maillard had been her guardian, but it was to Fell that she had always come with her girlish cares and troubles, during even the lifetime of her father. She had known Fell all her life; she had met him in strange places, both at home and abroad. She entertained a well-grounded suspicion that Jachin Fell had loved her mother, and this one fact lay between them, never mentioned but always there, like a bond of faith and kindliness.

At precisely three o'clock of the Sunday afternoon Jachin Fell rang the doorbell and Lucie herself admitted him. She ushered him into the parlour that was restful with its quiet brasses and old rosewood.

"Tell me quickly, Uncle Jachin!" eagerly exclaimed the girl. "Did you actually see the Midnight Masquer last night? I didn't know until afterward that he had really been downstairs and had robbed——"

"I saw him, my dear," and the little gray man smiled. There was more warmth to his smile than usual just now. Perhaps it was a reflection from the eager vitality which so shone in the eyes of Lucie. "I saw him, yes."

A restful face was hers—not beautiful at first glance; a little too strong for beauty one would say. The deep gray eyes were level and quiet and wide apart, and on most occasions were quite inscrutable. They were now filled with a quick eagerness as they rested upon Jachin Fell. Lucie called him uncle, but not as she called Joseph Maillard uncle; here was no relationship, no formal affectation of relationship, but a purely abiding trust and friendship.

Jachin Fell had done more for Lucie than she herself knew or would know; without her knowledge he had quietly taken care of her finances to an appreciable extent. Between them lay an affection that was very real. Lucie, better than most, knew the extraordinary capabilities of this little gray man; yet not even Lucie guessed a tenth of the character that lay beneath his surface. To her he was never reserved or secretive. Nonetheless, she touched sometimes an impenetrable wall that seemed ever present within him.

"You saw him?" repeated the girl, quickly. "What was he like? Do you know who he is?"

"Certainly I know," replied Fell, still smiling at her.

"Oh! Then who is he?"

"Softly, softly, young lady! I know him, but even to you I dare not breathe his name until I obtain some direct evidence. Let us call him Mr. X., after the approved methods of romance, and I shall expound what I know."

He groped in his vest pocket. Lucie sprang up, bringing a smoking stand from the corner of the room to his chair. She held a match to his El Rey, and then curled up on a Napoleon bed and watched him intently while he spoke.

"The bandit did not enter the house during the evening, nor did he leave, nor was he found in the house afterward," he said, tonelessly. "So, incredible as it may appear, he was one of the guests. This Mr. X. came to the dance wearing the aviator's costume, or most of it, underneath his masquerade costume. When he was ready to act, he doffed his outer costume, appeared as the Midnight Masquer, effected his purpose, then calmly donned his outer costume again and resumed his place among the guests. You understand?

"Well, then! Maillard yesterday received a note from the Masquer, brazenly stating that he intended to call during the evening. I have that note. It was written with an extremely hard lead pencil, such as few men carry, because it does not easily make very legible writing. Last night I asked Mr. X. for a pencil, and he produced one with an extra hard lead—mentioning that he had borrowed it from Bob Maillard, as indeed he had."

"What! Surely, you don't mean——"

"Of course I don't. Mr. X. is very clever, that's all. Here is what took place last night. Mr. X. brought us another note from the Masquer, saying that he had found it pinned to the library door. As a matter of fact, he had written it on a leaf torn from his notebook. I took the note from him, observing at the time that the paper had no pin holes. Probably, Mr. X. saw that there was something amiss; he presently went back downstairs, took the remainder of the torn leaf from his notebook, and pinned it to the door. A little later, I met him and mentioned the lack of pin holes; he calmly referred me to the piece on the door, saying that he had merely torn off the note without removing the pins. You follow me?"

"Of course," murmured the girl, her eyes wide in fascinated interest. "And he knew that you guessed him to be the Masquer?"

"He suspected me, I think," said Fell, mildly. "It is understood that you will not go about tracing these little clues? I do not wish to disclose his identity, even to your very discreet brain——"

"Don't be silly, Uncle Jachin!" she broke in. "You know I'll do nothing of the sort. Go on, please! Did you find the airplane?"

"Yes." Jachin Fell smiled drily. "I was thinking of that as I left the house and came to the line of waiting automobiles. A word with one of the outside detectives showed me that one of the cars in the street had been testing its engine about midnight. I found that the car belonged to Mr. X.

"How simple, Lucie, and how very clever! The chauffeur worked a powerful motor with a muffler cutout at about the time Mr. X., inside the house, was making his appearance. It scarcely sounded like an airplane motor, yet frightened and startled, people would imagine that it did. Thus arose the legend that the Midnight Masquer came and departed by means of airplane—a theory aided ingeniously by his costume. Well, that is all I know or suspect, my dear Lucie! And now——"

"Now, I suppose," said the girl, thoughtfully, "you'll put that awful Creole of yours on the track of Mr. X.? Ben Chacherre is a good chauffeur, and he's amusing enough—but he's a bloodhound! I don't wonder that he used to be a criminal. Even if you have rescued him from a life of crime, you haven't improved his looks."

"Exactly—Ben is at work," assented Jachin Fell. "The gentleman under suspicion is very prominent. To accuse him without proof would be utter folly. To catch him *in flagrante delicto* will be difficult. So, I am in no haste. He will not disappear, believe me, and something may turn up at any moment to undo him. Besides, I can as yet discover no motive for his crimes, since he is quite well off financially."

"Gambling," suggested the girl.

"I cannot find that he has lost any considerable sums. Well, no matter! Now that I have fully unbosomed myself, my dear, it is your turn."

"All right, Uncle Jachin." Lucie took a large morocco case from the chair beside her, and extended it. "You lent me these things to wear last night, and I——"

"No, no," intervened Fell. "I gave them to you, my dear—in fact, I bought them for you two years ago, and kept them until now! You have worn them; they are yours, and you become them better than even did poor Queen Hortense! So say no more. I trust that Mrs. Maillard was righteous and envious?"

"She was disagreeable," said Lucie. She leaned forward and imprinted a kiss upon the cheek of the little gray man. "There! that is all the thanks I can give you, dear uncle; the gift makes me very happy, and I'll not pretend otherwise. Only, I feel as though I had no right to wear them—they're so wonderful!"

"Nonsense! You can do anything you want to, as Eliza said when she crossed the ice. But all this isn't why you summoned me here, you bundle of mystery! What bothered you last night, or rather, who?"

Lucie laughed. "There was a Franciscan who tried to be very mysterious, and to read my mind. He talked about oil, about a grasping, hard man, and mentioned you as my friend. Then he warned me against a proposal that Bob might make; and sure enough, Bob did propose to buy what land is left to me on Bayou Terrebonne, saying he'd persuade his oil company that there was oil on it, and that they'd buy or lease it. I told him no. The Franciscan, afterward, proved to be Henry Gramont; I wondered if you had mentioned——"

"Heaven forbid!" exclaimed Mr. Fell, piously. "I never even met Gramont until last night! Do you like him?"

"Very much." The girl's eyes met his frankly. "Do you?"

"Very much," said Jachin Fell.

Lucie's gray eyes narrowed, searched his face. "I'm almost able to tell when you're lying," she observed, calmly. "You said that a trifle too hastily, Uncle Jachin. Why don't you like him?"

Fell laughed, amused. "Perhaps I have a prejudice against foreign nobles, Lucie. Our own aristocracy is bad enough, but——"

"He's discarded all that. He was never French except in name."

"You speak as though you'd known him for some time. Have you had secrets from me?"

"I have!" laughter dimpled in the girl's face. "For years and years! When I was in New York with father, before the war, we met him; he was visiting in Newport with college friends. Then, you know that father and I were in France when the war broke out—father was ill and almost helpless at the time, you remember. Gramont came to Paris to serve with his regiment, and met us there. He helped us get away, procured real money for us, got us passage to New York. He knows lots of our friends, and I've always been deeply grateful to him for his assistance then.

"We've corresponded quite frequently during the war," she pursued. "I mentioned him several times after we got home from France, but you probably failed to notice the name. It's only since he came to New Orleans that I really kept any secrets from you; this time, I wanted to find out if you liked him."

Jachin Fell nodded slowly. His face was quite innocent of expression.

"Yes, yes," he said. "Yes—of course. He's a geologist or engineer, I think?"

"Both, and a good one. He's a stockholder in Bob Maillard's oil company, and I think he's come here to stay. Well, about last night—he probably guessed at some of my private affairs; I've written or spoken rather frankly, perhaps. Also, Bob may have blabbed to him. Bob still drinks—prohibition has not hit *him* very hard!"

"No," agreed Fell, gravely. "Unfortunately, no. Lucie, I've discovered a most important fact. Joseph Maillard did not own any stock in the Bayou Oil Company at the time your land was sold them by him, and he had no interest at all in the real estate concern that bought your St. Landry swamplands and made a fortune off them. We have really blamed him most unjustly."

For a moment there was silence between them.

"We need not mince matters," pursued Fell, slowly. "Maillard has no scruples and no compassion; all the same, I am forced to the belief that he has maintained your interest uprightly, and that his mistakes were only errors. I do not believe that he has profited in the least from you. Two small fortunes were swept out of your grip when he sold those lands; yet they had been worthless, and he had good offers for them. His investments in the companies concerned were made afterward, and I am certain he sold the lands innocently."

Lucie drew a deep breath.

"I am glad you have said this," she returned, simply. "It's been hard for me to think that Uncle Joseph had taken advantage of me; I simply couldn't make myself believe it. I think that he honestly likes me, as far as he permits himself to like any one."

"He'd not loan you money on it," said Fell. "Friendship isn't a tangible security with him. And a girl is never secure, as Eliza said when she crossed the ice."

"Well, who really did profit by my loss? Any one?"

Fell's pale gray eyes twinkled, then cleared in their usually wide innocence.

"My dear Lucie, is there one person in this world to whose faults Joseph Maillard is deliberately blind—one person to whose influence he is ever open—one person to whom he would refuse nothing, in whom he would pardon everything, of whom he would never believe any evil report?"

"You mean——" Lucie drew a quick breath, "Bob?"

"Yes, I mean Bob. That he has profited by your loss I am not yet in a position to say; but I suspect it. He has his father's cupidity without his father's sense of honour to restrain him. When I have finished with the Masquer, I shall take up his trail."

Jachin Fell rose. "Now I must be off, my dear. By the way, if I have need of you in running down the Masquer, may I call upon your services?"

"Certainly! I'd love to help, Uncle Jachin! We'd be real detectives?"

"Almost." Jachin Fell smiled slightly. "Will you dine with us to-morrow evening, Lucie? My mother commanded me to bring you as soon as possible——"

"Oh, your mother!" exclaimed the girl, contritely. "I was so absorbed in the Masquer that I forgot to ask after her. How is she?"

"Quite as usual, thank you. I presume that you'll attend Comus with the Maillards?"

"Yes. I'll come to-morrow night gladly, Uncle Jachin."

"And we'll take a look at the Proteus ball afterward, if you like. I'll send Ben Chacherre for you with the car, if you're not afraid of him."

Lucie looked gravely into the smiling eyes of Fell.

"I'm not exactly afraid of him," she responded, soberly, "but there is something about him that I can't like. I'm sorry that you're trying to regenerate him, in a way."

Fell shrugged lightly. "All life is an effort, little one! Well, good-bye."

Jachin Fell left the house at three-forty. Twenty minutes later the bell rang again. Lucie sent one of the servants to admit Henry Gramont; she kept him waiting a full fifteen minutes before she appeared, and then she made no apologies whatever for the delay.

Not that Gramont minded waiting; he deemed it a privilege to linger in this house! He loved to study the place, so reflective of its owner. He loved the white Colonial mantel that surrounded the fireplace, perpetually alight, with its gleaming sheen of old brasses, and the glittering fire-set to one side. The very air of the place, the atmosphere that it breathed, was sweet to him.

The Napoleon bed that filled the bow window, with its pillows and soft coverings; the inlaid walnut cabinet made by Sheraton, with its quaintly curved glasses that reflected the old-time curios within; the tilt tables, the rosewood chairs, the rugs, bought before the oriental rug market was flooded with machine-made Senna knots— about everything here had an air of comfort, of long use, of restfulness. It was not the sort of place built up, raw item by raw item, by the colour-frenzied hands of decorators. It was the sort of place that decorators strive desperately to imitate, and cannot.

When Lucie made her appearance, Gramont bent over her hand and addressed her in French.

"You are charming as ever, Shining One! And in years to come you will be still more charming. That is the beauty of having a name taken direct from the classics and bestowed as a good fairy's gift——"

"Thank you, monsieur—but you have translated my name at least twenty times, and I am weary of hearing it," responded Lucie, laughingly.

"Poor taste, mademoiselle, to grow weary of such beauty!"

"Not of the name, but of your exegesis upon it. Why should I not be displeased? Last night you were positively rude, and now you decry my taste! Did you leave all your manners in France, M. le prince?"

"Some of them, yes—and all that prince stuff with them." Smiling as he dropped into English, Gramont glanced about the room, and his eyes softened.

"This is a lovey and loveable home of yours, Lucie!" he exclaimed, gravely. "So few homes are worthy the name;

so few have in them the intimate air of use and friendliness—why are so many furnished from bargain sales? This place is touched with repose and sweetness; to come and sit here is a privilege. It is like being in another world, after all the money striving and the dollar madness of the city."

"Oh!" The girl's gaze searched him curiously. "I hope you're not going to take the fine artistic pose that it is a crime to make money?"

Gramont laughed.

"Not much! I want to make money myself; that's one reason I'm in New Orleans. Still, you cannot deny that there is a craze about the eternal clutching after dollars. I can't make the dollar sign the big thing in life, Lucie. You couldn't, either."

She frowned a little.

"You seem to have the European notion that all Americans are dollar chasers!"

He shrugged his shoulders slightly. His harshly lined face was very strong; one sensed that its harshness had come from the outside—from hunger, from hardship and privations, from suffering strongly borne. He had not gone through the war unscathed, this young man who had tossed away a princely "de" in order to become plain Henry Gramont, American citizen.

"In a sense, yes; why not?" he answered. "I am an American. I am a dollar chaser, and not ashamed of it. I am going into business here. Once it is a success, I shall go on; I shall see America, I shall come to know this whole country of mine, all of it! I have been a month in New Orleans—do you know, a strange thing happened to me only a few days after I arrived here!"

With her eyes she urged him on, and he continued gravely:

"In France I met a man, an American sergeant named Hammond. It was just at the close of things. We had adjoining cots at Nice——"

"Ah!" she exclaimed, quickly. "I remember, you wrote about him—the man who had been wounded in both legs! Did he get well? You never said."

"I never knew until I came here," answered Gramont. "One night, not long after I had got established in my pension on Burgundy Street, a man tried to rob me. It was this same man, Hammond; we recognized each other almost at once.

"I took him home with me and learned his story. He had come back to America only to find his wife dead from influenza, his home broken up, his future destroyed. He drifted to New Orleans, careless of what happened to him. He flung himself desperately into a career of burglary and pillage. Well, I gave Hammond a job; he is my chauffeur. You would never recognize him as the same man now! I am very proud of his friendship."

"That was well said." Lucie nodded her head quickly. "I shan't call you M. Le prince any more—unless you offend again."

He smiled, reading her thought. "I try not to be a snob, eh? Well, what I'm driving at is this: I want to know this country of mine, to see it with clear, unprejudiced eyes. We hide our real shames and exalt our false ones. Why should we be ashamed of chasing the dollar? So long as that is a means to the end of happiness, it's all right. But there are some men who see it as an end alone, who can set no *finis* to their work except the dollar dropping into their pouch. Such a man is your relative, Joseph Maillard—I say it without offence."

Lucie nodded, realizing that he was driving at some deeper thing, and held her peace.

"You realize the fact, eh?" Gramont smiled faintly. "I do not wish to offend you, and I shall therefore refrain from saying all that is in my mind. But you have not hesitated to intimate very frankly that you are not wealthy. Some time ago, if you recall, you wrote me how you had just missed wealth through having sold some land. I have taken the liberty of looking up that deal to some extent, and I have suspected that your uncle had some interest in putting the sale through——"

The gray eyes of the girl flashed suddenly.

"Henry Gramont! Are my family affairs to be an open book to the world?" A slight flush, perhaps of anger, perhaps of some other emotion, rose in the girl's cheeks. "Do you realize that you are intruding most unwarrantably into my private matters?"

"Unwarrantably?" Gramont's eyes held her gaze steadily. "Do you really mean to use that word?"

"I do, most certainly!" answered Lucie with spirit. "I don't think you realize just what the whole thing tends toward——"

"Oh, yes I do! Quite clearly." Gramont's cool, level tone conquered her indignation. "I see that you are orphaned, and that your uncle was your guardian, and executed questionable deals which lost money for you. Come, that's brutally frank—but it's true! We are friends of long standing; not intimate friends, perhaps, and yet I think very good friends. I am most certainly not ashamed to say that when I had the occasion to look out for your interests I was very glad of the chance."

Gramont paused, but she did not speak. He continued after a moment:

"You had intimated to me, perhaps without meaning to do so, something of the situation. I came here to New Orleans and became involved in some dealings with your cousin, Bob Maillard. I believed, and I believe now, that in your heart you have some suspicion of your uncle in regard to those transactions in land. Therefore, I took the trouble to look into the thing to a slight extent. Shall I tell you what I have discovered?"

Lucie Ledanois gazed at him, her lips compressed. She liked this new manner of his, this firm and resolute gravity, this harshness. It brought out his underlying character very well.

"If you please, Henry," she murmured very meekly. "Since you have thrust yourself into my private affairs, I think I should at least get whatever benefit I can!"

"Exactly. Why not?" He made a grave gesture of assent. "Well, then, I have discovered that your uncle appears to be honestly at fault in the matter——"

"Thanks for this approval of my family," she murmured.

"And," continued Gramont, imperturbably, "that your suspicions of him were groundless. But, on the other hand, something new has turned up about which I wish to speak—but about which I must speak delicately."

"Be frank, my dear Henry—even brutal! Speak, by all means."

"Very well. Has Bob Maillard offered to buy your remaining land on the Bayou Terrebonne?"

She started slightly. So it was to this that he had been leading up all the while!

"He broached the subject last night," she answered. "I dismissed it for the time."

"Good!" he exclaimed with boyish vigour. "Good! I warned you in time, then! If you will permit me, I must advise you not to part with that land—not even for a good offer. This week, immediately Mardi Gras is over, I am going to inspect that land for the company; it is Bob Maillard's company, you know.

"If there's any chance of finding oil there, I shall first see you, then advise the company. You can hold out for your fair share of the mineral rights, instead of selling the whole thing. You'll get it! Landowners around here are not yet wise to the oil game, but they'll soon learn."

"You would betray your business associates to help me?" she asked, curious to hear his reply. A slow flush crept into his cheeks.

"Certainly not! But I would not betray you to help my business friends. Is my unwarrantable intrusion forgiven?"

She nodded brightly. "You are put on probation, sir. You're in Bob's company?"

"Yes." Gramont frowned. "I invested perhaps too hastily—but no matter now. I have the car outside, Lucie; may I have the pleasure of taking you driving?"

"Did you bring that chauffeur?"

"Yes," and he laughed at her eagerness.

"Good! I accept—because I must see that famous soldier-bandit-chauffeur. If you'll wait, I'll be ready in a minute."

She hurried from the room, a snatch of song on her lips. Gramont smiled as he waited.

Chapter 5: The Masquer Unmasks

In New Orleans one may find pensions in the old quarter—the quarter which is still instinct with the pulse of old-world life. These pensions do not advertise. The average tourist knows nothing of them. Even if he knew, indeed, he might have some difficulty in obtaining accommodations, for it is not nearly enough to have the money; one must also have the introductions, come well recommended, and be under the tongue of good repute.

Gramont had obtained a small apartment *en pension*—a quiet and severely retired house in Burgundy Street, maintained by a very proud old lady whose ancestors had come out of Canada with the Sieur d'Iberville. Here Gramont lived with Hammond, quite on a basis of equality, and they were very comfortable.

The two men sat smoking their pipes before the fireplace, in which blazed a small fire—more for good cheer than through necessity. It was Sunday evening. Between Gramont and Hammond had arisen a discussion regarding their relations—a discussion which was perhaps justified by Gramont's quixotic laying down of the law.

"It's all very well, Hammond," he mused, "to follow custom and precedent, to present to the world a front which will not shock its proprieties, its sense of tradition and fitness. In the world's eye you are my chauffeur. But when we're alone together—nonsense!"

"That's all right, cap'n," said Hammond, shrewdly. To him, Gramont was always "cap'n" and nothing else. "But you know's well as I do it can't go on forever. I'm workin' for you, and that's the size of it. I ain't got the education to stack up alongside of you. I don't want you to get the notion that I'm figuring on takin' advantage of you——"

"Bosh! I suppose some day I'll be wealthy, married, and bound in the chains of social usage and custom," said Gramont, energetically. "But that day isn't here yet. If you think I'll accept deference and servility from any man who has endured the same hunger and cold and wounds that I endured in France—then guess again! We're friends in a democracy of Americans. You're just as good a man as I am, and vice versa. Besides, aren't we fellow criminals?"

Hammond grinned at this. There was no lack of shrewd intelligence in his broad and powerful features, which were crowned by a rim of reddish hair.

"All that line o' bull sounds good, cap'n, only it's away off," he returned. "Trouble with you is, you ain't forgot the war yet."

"I never will," said Gramont, his face darkening.

"Sure you will! We all will. And you ain't as used to this country as I am, either. I've seen too much of it. You ain't seen enough."

"I've seen enough to know that it's my country."

"Right. But I ain't as good a man as you are, not by a long shot!" said Hammond, cheerfully. "You proved that the night you caught me comin' into the window at the Lavergne house. You licked me without half tryin', cap'n!

"Anyhow," pursued Hammond, "America ain't a democracy, unless you're runnin' for Congress. It sounds good to the farmers, but wait till you've been here long enough to get out of your fine notions! Limousines and money ain't got much use for democracy. The men who have brains, like you, always will give orders, I reckon."

"Bosh!" said Gramont again. "It isn't a question of having brains. It's a question of knowing what to do with them. All men are born free and equal——"

"Not much!" retorted the other with conviction. "All men were born free, but mighty few were born equal, cap'n. That sort o' talk sounds good in the newspapers, but it don't go very far with the guy at the bottom, nor the top, either!"

Gramont stared into the flickering fire and sucked at his pipe. He realized that in a sense Hammond was quite correct in his argument; nonetheless, he looked on the other man as a comrade, and always would do so. It was true that he had not forgotten the war. Suddenly he roused himself and shot a glance at Hammond.

"Sergeant! You seem to have a pretty good recollection of that night at the Lavergne house, when I found you entering and jumped on you."

"You bet I have!" Hammond chuckled. "When you'd knocked the goggles off me and we recognized each other—hell! I felt like a boob."

Gramont smiled. "How many places had you robbed up to then? Three, wasn't it?"

"Three is right, cap'n," was the unashamed response.

"We haven't referred to it very often, but now things have happened." Gramont's face took on harsh lines of determination. "Do you know, it was a lucky thing that you had no chance to dispose of the jewels and money you obtained? But I suppose you didn't call it good luck at the time."

"No chance?" snorted the other. "No chance is right, cap'n! And I was sore, too. Say, they got a ring of crooks around this town you couldn't bust into with grenades! I couldn't figure it out for a while, but only the other day I got the answer. Listen here, and I'll tell you something big."

Hammond leaned forward, lowered his voice, and tamped at his pipe.

"When I was a young fellow I lived in a little town up North—I ain't sayin' where. My old man had a livery stable there, see? Well, one night a guy come along and got the old man out of bed, and slips him fifteen hundred for a rig and a team, see? I drove the guy ten miles through the hills, and set him on a road he wanted to find.

"Now, that guy was the biggest crook in the country in them days—still is, I guess. He was on the dead run that night, to keep out o' Leavenworth. He kep' out, all right, and he's settin' in the game to this minute. Nobody never pinched him yet, and never will."

Gramont's face had tensed oddly as he listened. Now he shot out a single word:

"Why?"

"Because his gang runs back to politicians and rich guys all over the country. You ask anybody on the inside if they ever heard of Memphis Izzy Gumberts! Well, cap'n, I seen that very identical guy on the street the other day—I never could forget his ugly mug! And where *he* is, no outside crooks can get in, you believe me!"

"Hm! Memphis Izzy Gumberts, eh? What kind of a crook is he, sergeant?"

"The big kind. You remember them Chicago lotteries? But you don't, o' course. Well, that's his game—lotteries and such like."

Gramont's lips clenched for a minute, then he spoke with slow distinctness:

"Sergeant, I'd have given five hundred dollars for that information a week ago!"

"Why?" Hammond stared at him suddenly. Gramont shook his head.

"Never mind. Forget it! Now, this stunt of yours was clever. You showed brains when you got yourself up as an aviator and pulled that stuff, sergeant. But you handled it brutally—terribly brutally."

"It was a little raw, I guess," conceded Hammond. "I was up against it, that's all—I figured they'd pinch me sooner or later, but I didn't care, and that's the truth! I was out for the coin.

"When you took over the costume and began to get across with the Raffles stuff—why, it was a pipe for you, cap'n! Look what we've done in a month. Six jobs, every one running off smooth as glass! Your notion of going to parties ready dressed with some kind of loose robe over the flyin' duds was a scream! And then me running that motor with the cutout on—all them birds that never heard an airplane think you come and go by air, for certain! I will say that I ain't on to why you're doing it; just the same, you've got them all fooled, and I ain't worried a particle about the cops or the crooks, either one. But watch out for the Gumberts crowd! They're liable to show us up to the bulls, simply because we ain't in with 'em. Nobody else will ever find us out."

Gramont nodded thoughtfully.

"Yes? But, sergeant, how about the quiet little man who came along last night at the Maillard house and asked about the car? Perhaps he had discovered you had been running the engine."

"Him?" Hammond sniffed in scorn. "He wasn't no dick."

"Well, I was followed to-day; at least, I think I was. I could spot nobody after me, but I felt certain of it. And let me tell you something about that same quiet little man! His name is Jachin Fell."

"Heluva name," commented Hammond, and wrinkled up his brow. "Jachin, huh? Seems like I've heard the name before. Out o' the Bible, ain't it? Something about Jachin and Boaz?"

"I imagine so." Gramont smiled as he replied. "Fell is a lawyer, but he never practises law. He's rich, he's a very fine chess player—and probably the smartest man in New Orleans, sergeant. Just what he does I don't know; no one does. I imagine that he's one of those quiet men who stay in the backgrounds of city politics and pull the strings. You know, one administration has been in power here for nearly twenty years—it's something to make a man stop and think!

"This chap Fell is sharp, confoundedly sharp!" went on Gramont, while the chauffeur listened with frowning intentness. "He's altogether too sharp to be a criminal— or I'd suspect that he was using his knowledge of the law to beat the law. Well, I think that he is on to me, and is trying to get the goods on me."

"Oh!" said Hammond. "And someone was trailin' you? Think he's put the bulls wise?"

Gramont shrugged his shoulders. "I don't know. He almost caught me last night. We'll have to get rid of that aviator's suit at once, and of the loot also. I suppose you've reconciled yourself to returning the stuff?"

Hammond stirred uneasily, and laid down his pipe.

"Look here, cap'n," he said, earnestly. "I wasn't runnin' a holdup game because I liked it, and I wasn't doing it for the fun of the thing, like you are. I was dead broke, I hadn't any hope left, and I didn't care a damn whether I lived or died—that's on the dead! Right there, you come along and picked me up.

"You give me a job. What's more, you've treated me white, cap'n. I guess you seen that I was just a man with the devil at his heels, and you chased the devil off. You've given me something decent to live for—to make good because you got some faith in me! Why, when you went out on that first job of ours, d'you know it like to broke me up? It did. Only, when we got home that night and you said it was all a joke, and you'd send back the loot later on, then I begun to feel better about it. Even if you'd gone into it as a reg'lar business, I'd have stuck with you—but I was darned glad about its bein' a joke!"

Gramont nodded in comprehension of the other's feeling.

"It's not been altogether a joke, sergeant," he said, gravely. "To tell the truth, I did start it as a joke, but soon afterward I learned something that led me to keep it up. I kept it up until I could hit the Maillard house. It was my intention to turn up at the Comus ball, on Tuesday night, and there make public restitution of the stuff—but that's impossible now. I dare not risk it! That man Fell is too smart."

"You're not goin' to pull the trick again, then?" queried Hammond, eagerly.

"No. I'm through. I've got what I wanted. Still, I don't wish to return the stuff before Wednesday—Ash

Wednesday, the end of the carnival season. Suppose you get out the loot and find me some boxes. And be sure they have no name on them or any store labels."

Hammond leaped up and vanished in the room adjoining. Presently he returned, bearing several cardboard boxes which he dumped on the centre table. Gramont examined them closely, and laid aside a number that were best suited to his purpose. Meantime, the chauffeur was opening a steamer trunk which he pulled from under the bed.

"I'm blamed glad you're done, believe me!" he uttered, fervently, glancing up at Gramont. "Far's I'm concerned I don't care much, but I'd sure hate to see the bulls turn in a guy like you, cap'n. You couldn't ever persuade anybody that it was all a joke, neither, once they nabbed you. They're a bad bunch o' bulls in this town—it ain't like Chi or other places, where you can stand in right and do a bit o' fixing."

"You seem to know the game pretty well," and Gramont smiled amusedly.

"Ain't I been a chauffeur and garage man?" retorted Hammond, as though this explained much. "If there's anything us guys don't run up against, you can't name it! Here we are. Want me to keep each bunch separate, don't you?"

"Sure. I'll be writing some notes to go inside."

Gramont went to a buhl writing desk in the corner of the room, and sat down. He took out his notebook, tore off several sheets, and from his pocket produced a pencil having an extremely hard lead. He wrote a number of notes, which, except for the addresses, were identical in content:

DEAR SIR:
I enclose herewith certain jewellery and articles, also currency, recently obtained by me under your kind auspices.

I trust that you will assume the responsibility of returning these things to the various guests who lost them while under your roof. I regret any discomfort occasioned by my taking them as a loan, which I now return. Please convey to the several owners my profound esteem and my assurance that I shall not in future appear to trouble any one, the carnival season having come to an end, and with it my little jest.

THE MIDNIGHT MASQUER.

Gathering up these notes in his hand, Gramont went to the fireplace. He tossed the pencil into the fire, following it with the notebook.

"Can't take chances with that man Fell," he explained. "All ready, sergeant. Let's go down the list one by one."

From the trunk Hammond produced ticketed packages, which he placed on the table. Gramont selected one, opened it, carefully packed the contents in one of the boxes, placed the proper addressed note on top, and handed it to the chauffeur.

"Wrap it up and address it. Give the return address of John Smith, Bayou Teche."

One by one they went through the packages of loot in the same manner. Before them on the table, as they worked, glittered little heaps of rings, brooches, watches, currency; jewels that flashed garishly with coloured fires, historic and famous jewels plucked from the aristocratic heart of the southland, heirlooms of a past generation side by side with platinum crudities of the present fashion.

There had been heartburnings in the loss of these things, Gramont knew. He could picture to himself something of what had followed his robberies: family quarrels, new purchases in the gem marts, bitter reproaches, fresh mortgages on old heritages, vexations of wealthy dowagers, shrugs of unconcern by the *nouveaux riches*; perchance lives altered—deaths—divorces——

"There's a lot of human life behind these baubles, sergeant," he reflected aloud, a cold smile upon his lips as he worked. "When they come back to their owners, I'd like to be hovering around in an invisible mantle to watch results! Could we only know it, we're probably affecting the lives of a great many people—for good and ill. These things stand for money; and there's nothing like money, or the lack of it, to guide the destinies of people."

"You said it," and Hammond grinned. "I'm here to prove it, ain't I? I ain't pulling no more gunplay, now I got me a steady job."

"And a steady friend, old man," added Gramont. "Did it occur to you that maybe I was as much in need of a friend as you were?"

He had come to the last box now, that which must go to Joseph Maillard. On top of the money and scarfpins which he placed in the box he laid a thin packet of papers. He tapped them with his finger.

"Those papers, sergeant! To get them, I've been playing the whole game. To get them and not to let their owner suspect that I was after them! Now they're going back to their owner."

"Who's he?" demanded Hammond.

"Young Maillard—son of the banker. He roped me into an oil company; caught me, like a sucker, almost the first week I was here. I put pretty near my whole wad into that company of his."

"You mean he stung you?"

"Not yet." Gramont smiled coldly, harshly. "That was his intention; he thought I was a Frenchman who would fall for any sort of game. I fell right enough—but I'll come out on top of the heap."

The other frowned. "I don't get you, cap'n. Some kind o' stock deal?"

"Yes, and no." Gramont paused, and seemed to choose his words with care. "Miss Ledanois, the lady who was driving with us this afternoon, is an old friend of mine. I've known for some time that somebody was fleecing her.

I suspected that it was Maillard the elder, for he has had the handling of her affairs for some time past. Now, however, those papers have given me the truth. He was straight enough with her; his son was the man.

"The young fool imagines that by trickery and juggling he is playing the game of high finance! He worked on his father, made his father sell land owned by Miss Ledanois, and he himself reaped the profits. There are notes and stock issues among those papers that give his whole game away, to my eyes. Not legal evidence, as I had hoped, but evidence enough to show me the truth of things—to show me that he's a scoundrel! Further, they bear on my own case, and I'm satisfied now that I'd be ruined if I stayed with him."

"Well, that's easy settled," said Hammond. "Just hold him up with them papers—make him come across!"

"I'm not in that sort of business. I stole those papers, not to use them for blackmail, but to get information. By the way, get that tin box out of my trunk, will you? I want to take my stock certificates with me in the morning, and must not forget them."

Hammond disappeared into the adjoining room.

Gramont sat gazing at the boxes before him. Despite his words to Hammond, there was a fund of puzzled displeasure in his eyes, sheer dissatisfaction. He shook his head gloomily, and his eyes clouded.

"All wasted—the whole effort!" he murmured. "I thought it might lead to something, but all it has given me is the reward of saving myself and possibly retrieving Lucie. As for the larger game, the bigger quarry—it's all wasted. I haven't unravelled a single thread; the first real clue came to me to-night, purely by accident. Memphis Izzy Gumberts! That's the lead to follow! I'll get rid of this Midnight Masquer foolishness and go after the real game."

Gramont was to discover that it is not nearly so easy to be rid of folly as it is to don the jester's cap and bells; a fact which one Simplicissimus had discovered to his sorrow three hundred years earlier. But, as Gramont was not versed in this line of literature, he yet had the discovery ahead of him.

Hammond reentered the room with the tin box, from which Gramont took his stock certificates issued by Bob Maillard's oil company. He pocketed the shares.

"Does this here Miss Ledanois," asked Hammond, "play in with you in the game? Young Maillard's related to her, ain't he?"

"She's quite aware of his drawbacks, I think," answered Gramont, drily.

"I see." Hammond rubbed his chin, and inspected his employer with a twinkle denoting perfect comprehension. "Well, how d'you expect to come out on top of the heap?"

"I want to get my own money back," explained Gramont. "You see, young Maillard thinks that he's cleaned me up fine. I've invested heavily in his company, which has a couple of small wells already going. As I conceive the probable scheme, this company is scheduled to fail, and another company will take over the stock at next to nothing. Maillard will be the other company; his present associates will be the suckers! It's that, or some similar trick. I'm no longer interested in the affair."

"Why not, if you got money in it?"

"My son, to-morrow is Monday. Proteus will arrive out of the sea to-morrow, and the Proteus ball comes off to-morrow night. In spite of these distractions, the banks are open in the morning. Savvy?

"I'll go to Maillard the banker—Joseph Maillard—first thing in the morning, and offer him my stock. He'll be mighty glad to get it at a discount, knowing that it is in his son's company. You see, the son doesn't confide in the old man particularly. I'll let the father win a little money on the deal with me, and by doing this I'll manage to save the greater part of my investment——"

"Holy mackerel!" Hammond exploded in a burst of laughter as he caught the idea. "Say, if this ain't the richest thing ever pulled! When the crash comes, the fancy kid will be stinging his dad good and hard, eh?"

"Exactly; and I think his dad can afford to be stung much better than I can," agreed Gramont, cheerfully. "Also, now that I'm certain Bob Maillard is the one who was behind the fleecing of Miss Ledanois, I'll first get clear of him, then I'll start to give him his deserts. I may form an oil company of my own."

"Do it," advised Hammond, still chuckling.

"Now," and Gramont rose, "let's take those packages and stow them away in the luggage compartment of the car. I'm getting nervous at the thought of having them around here, and they'll be perfectly safe there overnight—safer there than here, in fact. To-morrow, you can take the car out of town and send the packages by parcels post from some small town.

"In that way they ought to be delivered here on Wednesday. You'd better wear one of my suits, leaving your chauffeur's outfit here, and don't halt the car in front of the postoffice where you mail the packages——"

"I get you," assented Hammond, sagely. "I'll leave the car outside town, and hoof it in with the boxes, so that nobody will notice the car or connect it with the packages, eh? But what about them aviator's clothes?"

"Take them with you—better get them wrapped up here and now. You can toss them into a ditch anywhere."

Hammond obeyed.

Ten minutes afterward the two men left the room, carrying the packages of loot and the bundle containing the aviator's uniform. They descended to the courtyard in the rear of the house. Here was a small garden, with a fountain in its centre. Behind this were the stables, which had long been disused as such, and which were now occupied only by the car of Gramont.

It was with undisguised relief that Gramont now saw the stuff actually out of the house. Within the last few hours he had become intensely afraid of Jachin Fell. Concentrating himself upon the man, picking up information guardedly, he had that day assimilated many small items which increased his sense of peril from that quarter. Straws, no more, but quite significant straws. Gramont realized clearly that if the police ever searched his rooms and found this loot, he would be lost. There could be no excuse that would hold water for a minute against such evidence.

In the garage, Hammond switched on the lights of the car. By the glow they disposed their burdens in the luggage compartment of the tonneau, which held them neatly. The car was a large twelve-cylinder, four-passenger Nonpareil, which Gramont had picked up in the used-car market. Hammond had tinkered it into magnificent shape, and loved the piece of mechanism as the very apple of his eye.

The luggage compartment closed and locked, they returned into the house and dismissed the affair as settled.

Upon the following morning Gramont, who usually breakfasted *en pension* with his hostess, had barely seated himself at the table when he perceived the figure of Hammond at the rear entrance of the dining room. The chauffeur beckoned him hastily.

"Come out here, cap'n!" Hammond was breathing heavily, and seemed to be in some agitation. "Want to show you somethin'!"

"Is there anything important?" Gramont hesitated. The other regarded him with a baleful countenance.

"Important? Worse'n that!"

Gramont rose and followed Hammond out to the garage, much to his amazement. The chauffeur halted beside the car and extended him a key, pointing to the luggage compartment.

"Here's the key—you open her!"

"What's the matter, man?"

"The stuff's gone!"

Gramont seized the key and opened the compartment. It proved empty indeed. He stared up into the face of Hammond who was watching in dogged silence.

"I knew you'd suspect me," broke out the chauffeur, but Gramont interrupted him curtly.

"Don't be a fool; nothing of the sort. Was the garage locked?"

"Yes, and the compartment, too! I came out to look over that cut tire, and thought I'd make sure the stuff was safe——"

"We're up against it, that's all." Gramont compressed his lips for a moment. Then he straightened up and clapped the other on the shoulder. "Buck up! I never thought of suspecting you, old fellow. Someone must have been watching us last night, eh?"

"The guy that trailed you yesterday, most like," agreed Hammond, dourly. "It ain't hard to break into this place, and any one could open that compartment with a hairpin."

"Well, you're saved a trip into the country."

"You think they got us, cap'n? What can we do?"

"Do?" Gramont shrugged his shoulders and laughed. "Nothing except to wait and see what happens next! If you want to run, I'll give you enough money to land you in New York or Frisco——"

"Run—hell!" Hammond sniffed in scorn. "What d'you think I am—a boche? I'll stick."

"Good boy." Gramont turned toward the house. "Come along in and get breakfast, and don't touch that compartment door. I want to examine it later."

Hammond gazed admiringly after him as he crossed the garden. "If you ain't a cool hand, I'm a Dutchman!" he murmured, and followed his master.

Chapter 6: Chacherre

At ten o'clock that Monday morning Gramont's car approached Canal Street, and halted a block distant. For any car to gain Canal, much less to follow it, was impossible. From curb to curb the wide avenue was thronged with carnival folk, who would hold their own until Proteus came ashore to manage his own parade and his own section of the festivities.

Gramont left the car, and turned to speak with Hammond.

"I've made out at least two fingerprints on the luggage compartment," he said, quietly. "Drive around to police headquarters and enter a complaint in my name to a robbery of the compartment; say that the thief got away with some valuable packages I had been about to mail. They have a process of transferring fingerprints such as these; get it done. Perhaps they can identify the thief, for it must have been some clever picklock to get into the compartment without leaving a scratch. Take your time about it and come home when you've finished."

Hammond listened stolidly. "If it was the bulls done it, cap'n, going to them will get us pinched sure——"

"If they had done it," said Gramont, "we'd have been pinched long before this! It was someone sent by that devil Jachin Fell, and I'll land him if I can!"

"Then Fell will land us if he's got the stuff!"

"Let him! How can he prove anything, unless he had brought the police to open up that compartment? Get along with you!"

Hammond grinned, saluted, and drove away.

Slowly Gramont edged his way through the eddying crowds to Canal Street, and presently gained the imposing portals of the Exeter National Bank. Entering the building, he sent his card to the private office of the president; a moment later he was ushered in, and was closeted with Joseph Maillard.

The interior of the Exeter National reflected the stern personality that ruled it. The bank was dark, old fashioned, conservative, guarded with much effrontery of iron grills and bars against the evil doer.

The window men greeted their customers with infrequent smiles, with caution and reserve so great that it was positively chilly. Suspicion seemed in the air. The bank's reputation for guarding the sanctity of wealth seemed to rest heavily upon each pair of bowed shoulders. Even the stenographers were unhandsome women, weary-eyed, drearily efficient, and obviously respectable.

As befitted so old and conservative a New Orleans institution, much of its business was transacted in French.

The business customers of this bank found their affairs handled coldly, efficiently, with an inhuman precision that was admirable. It was good for business, and they liked it. There were no mistakes.

People who were accustomed to dealing with bankers of cordial smile and courteous word, people who liked to walk into a bank and to be met with a personal greeting, did not come here, nor were they wanted here. The Exeter National was a place for business, not for courtesy. It was absolutely precise, cold, inhuman, and spelled business from the ground up. Its oldest customer could not buy a draft on Paris or London or other of the bank's correspondents without paying the required fee. The wealthiest depositor could not expect to overdraw his checking account one dollar without being required to settle up before the next day was gone. Loans were made hesitatingly, grudgingly, and of necessity, always on security and never on character.

Such was the Exeter National. Its character was reflected in the cold faces at its windows, and the chance customers who entered its sacred portals were duly cowed and put in their proper place. Most of them were, that is. Occasionally some intrepid soul appeared who seemed impervious to the gloomy chill, who seemed even to resent it. One of these persons was now standing in the lobby and staring around with a cool impudence which drew unfavourable glances from the clerks.

He was a decently dressed fellow, obviously no customer of this sacrosanct place, obviously a stranger to its interior. Beneath a rakishly cocked soft hat beamed a countenance that bore a look of self-assured impertinent deviltry. After one look at that countenance the assistant cashier crooked a hasty finger at the floor guard, who nodded and walked over to the intruder with a polite query.

"Can I help you, sir?"

The intruder turned, favoured the guard with a cool stare, then broke into a laugh and a flood of Creole dialect.

"Why, if it isn't old Lacroix from Carencro! And look at the brass buttons—*diable*! You must own this place, hein? *la tche chatte pousse avec temps*—the cat's tail grows in time, I see! You remember me?"

"Ben Chacherre!" exclaimed the guard, losing his dignity for an instant. "Why—you *vaurien*, you! You who disappeared from the parish and became a vagrant——"

"So you turn up your sanctified nose at Ben Chacherre, do you?" exclaimed that person jauntily. He thrust his hat a bit farther over one ear, and proceeded to snap his fingers under the nose of Lacroix.

"A *vaurien*, am I? Old peacock! Lead me to the man who cashes checks, lackey, brass buttons that you are! Come, obey me, or I'll have you thrown into the street!"

"You—you wish to cash a check?" The guard was overcome by confusion, for the loud tones of Chacherre penetrated the entire institution. "But you are not known here——"

"Bah, insolent one! *Macaque dan calebasse*—monkey in the calabash that you are! Do you not know me?"

"Heaven preserve me! I will not answer for your accursed checks."

"Go to the devil, then," snapped Chacherre, and turned away.

His roving eyes had already found the correct window by means of the other persons seeking it, and now he stepped into the small queue that had formed. When it came his turn, he slid his check across the marble slab, tucked his thumbs into the armholes of his vest, and impudently stared into the questioning, coldly repellent eyes of the teller.

"Well?" he exclaimed, as the teller examined the check. "Do you wish to eat it, that you sniff so hard?"

The teller gave him a glance. "This is for a thousand dollars——"

"Can I not read?" said Chacherre, with an impudent gesture. "Am I an ignorant 'Cajun? Have I not eyes in my head? If you wish to start an argument, say that the check is for a hundred dollars. Then, by heaven, I will argue something with you!"

"You are Ben Chacherre, eh? Does any one here know you?"

Chacherre exploded in a violent oath. "Dolt that you are, do I have to be known when the check is endorsed under my signature? Who taught you business, monkey?"

"True," answered the teller, sulkily. "Yet the amount——"

"Oh, bah!" Chacherre snapped his fingers. "Go and telephone Jachin Fell, you old woman! Go and tell him you do not know his signature—well, who are you looking at? Am I a telephone, then? You are not hired to look but to act! Get about it."

The enraged and scandalized teller beckoned a confrere. Jachin Fell was telephoned. Presumably his response was reassuring, for Chacherre was presently handed a thousand dollars in small bills, as he requested. He insisted upon counting over the money at the window with insolent assiduity, flung a final compliment at the teller, and swaggered across the lobby. He was still standing by the entrance when Henry Gramont left the private office of the president and passed him by without a look.

Gramont was smiling to himself as he left the bank, and Ben Chacherre was whistling gaily as he also left and plunged into the whirling vortex of the carnival crowds.

Toward noon Gramont arrived afoot at his pension. Finding the rooms empty, he went on and passed through the garden. Behind the garage, in the alley, he discovered Hammond busily at work cleaning and polishing the engine of the car.

"Hello!" he exclaimed, cheerily. "What luck?"

"Pretty good, cap'n." Hammond glanced up, then paused.

A stranger was strolling toward them along the alleyway, a jaunty individual who was gaily whistling and who seemed entirely carefree and happy. He appeared to have no interest whatever in them, and Hammond concluded that he was innocuous.

"They got them prints fine, cap'n. What's more, they think they've located the fellow that made 'em."

"Ah, good work!" exclaimed Gramont. "Some criminal?"

Hammond frowned. The stranger had come to a halt a few feet distant, flung them a jerky, careless nod, and was beginning to roll a cigarette. He surveyed the car with a knowing and appreciative eye. Hammond turned his back on the man disdainfully.

"Yep—a sneak thief they'd pinched a couple of years back; didn't know where he was, but the prints seemed to fit him. They'll come up and look things over sometime to-day, then go after him and land him."

Gramont gave the stranger a glance, but the other was still surveying the car with evident admiration. If he heard their words he gave them no attention.

"Who was the man, then?" asked Gramont.

"A guy with a queer name—Ben Chacherre." Hammond pronounced it as he deemed correct—as the name was spelled. "Only they didn't call him that. Here, I wrote it down."

He fished in his pocket and produced a paper. Gramont glanced at it and laughed.

"Oh, Chacherre!" He gave the name the Creole pronunciation.

"Yep, Sasherry. I expect they'll come any time now—said two bulls would drop in."

"All right." Gramont nodded and turned away, with another glance at the stranger. "I'll not want the car to-day nor to-night that I know of. I'm not going to the Proteus ball. So your time's your own until to-morrow; make the most of it!"

He disappeared, and Hammond returned to his work. Then he straightened up, for the jaunty stranger was bearing down upon him with evident intent to speak.

"Some car you got there, brother!" Ben Chacherre, who had overheard most of the foregoing conversation, lighted his cigarette and grinned familiarly. "Some car, eh?"

"She's a boat, all right," conceded Hammond, grudgingly. He did not like the other's looks, although praise of the car was sweet unto his soul. "She sure steps some."

"Yes. All she needs," drawled Chacherre, "is some good tires, a new coat of paint, a good steel chassis, and a new engine——"

"Huh?" snorted Hammond. "Say, you 'bo, who sold you chips in this game? Move along!"

Ben grinned anew and rested himself against a near-by telephone pole.

"Free country, ain't it?" he inquired, lazily. "Or have you invested your winnings and bought this here alley?"

Hammond reddened with anger and took a step forward. The next words of Chacherre, however, jerked him sharply into self-control.

"Seen anything of an aviator's helmet around here?"

"Huh?" The chauffeur glared at his tormentor, yet with a sudden sick feeling inside his bosom. He suddenly realized that the man's eyes were meeting his squarely, with a bold and insolent directness. "Who you kiddin' now?"

"Nobody. I was asking a question, that's all." Ben Chacherre flung away his cigarette, untangled himself from the telephone pole, and moved away. "Only," he flung over his shoulder, "I was flyin' along here last night in my airplane, and I lost my helmet overboard. Thought maybe you'd seen it. So long, brother!"

Hammond stood staring after the swaggering figure; for once he was speechless. The jaunty words had sent terror thrilling into him. He started impulsively to pursue that impudent accoster—then he checked himself. Had the man guessed something? Had the man known something? Or had those words been only a bit of meaningless impertinence—a chance shaft which had accidentally flown home?

The last conjecture impressed itself on Hammond as being the truth, and his momentary fright died out. He concluded that the incident was not worth mentioning to Gramont, who surely had troubles enough of his own at this juncture. So he held his peace about it.

As for Ben Chacherre, he sauntered from the alley, a careless whistle upon his lips. Once out of Hammond's sight, however, he quickened his pace. Turning into a side street, he directed his step toward that part of the old quarter which, in the days before prohibition, had been given over to low cabarets and dives of various sorts. Most of these places were now boarded up, and presumably abandoned. Coming to one of them, which appeared more dirty and desolate than the rest, Chacherre opened a side door and vanished.

He entered what had once been the Red Cat cabaret. At a table in the half-darkened main room sat two men. A slovenly waiter pored over a newspaper at another table in a far corner. The two in the centre nodded to Chacherre. One of them, who was the proprietor, jerked his chin in an invitation to join them.

A man famous in the underworld circles, a man whose renown rested on curious feats and facts, this proprietor; few crooks in the country had not heard the name of Memphis Izzy Gumberts. He was a grizzled old bear now; but in times past he had been the head of a far-flung organization which, on each pay day, covered every army post in the country and diverted into its own pockets about two thirds of Uncle Sam's payroll—a feat still related in criminal circles as the *ne plus ultra* of success. Those palmy days were gone, but Memphis Izzy, who had never been "mugged" in any gallery, sat in his deserted cabaret and still did not lack for power and influence.

The man at his side was apparently not anxious to linger, for he rose and made his farewells as Chacherre approached.

"We have about eighteen cars left," he said to Gumberts. "Charley the Goog can attend to them, and the place is safe enough. They're up to you. I'm drifting back to Chi."

"Drift along," and Gumberts nodded, a leer in his eyes. His face was broad, heavy-jowled, filled with a keen and forceful craft. "It's a cinch that nobody in this state is goin' to interfere with us. About them cars from Texas— any news?"

"I've sent orders to bring 'em in next week."

Gumberts nodded again, and the man departed. Into the chair which he had vacated dropped Ben Chacherre, and took from his pocket the money which he had obtained at the bank. He laid it on the table before Gumberts.

"There you are," he said. "Amounts you want and all. The boss says to gimme a receipt."

"Wouldn't trust you, eh?" jeered Gumberts. He took out pencil and paper, scrawled a word or two, and shoved the paper at Chacherre. Then he reached down to a small satchel which lay open on the floor beside his chair. "Why wouldn't the boss leave the money come out of the takin's, hey?"

"Wanted to keep separate accounts," said Chacherre.

Gumberts nodded and produced two large sealed envelopes, which he pushed across the table.

"There's rakeoff for week before last," he announced. "Last week will be the big business, judgin' from early reports."

Chacherre pocketed the envelopes, lighted a cigarette, and leaned forward.

"Say, Izzy! You got to send a new man down to the Bayou Latouche right away. Lafarge was there, you know; a nigger shot him yesterday. The nigger threatened to squeal unless he got his money back—Lafarge was a fool and didn't know how to handle him. The lottery's goin' to get a bad name around there——"

Gumberts snapped his fingers. "Let it!" he said, calmly. "The big money from all that section is Chinese and Filipino, my friend. The niggers don't matter."

"Well, the boss says to shoot a new man down there. Also, he says, you'd better watch out about spreadin' the lottery into Texas and Alabama, account of the government rules."

The heavy features of Gumberts closed in a scowl.

"You tell your boss," he said, "that when it comes to steerin' clear of federal men, I don't want no instructions from nobody! We got every man in this state spotted. Every one that can be fixed is fixed—and that goes for the legislators and politicians clear up the line! Tell your boss to handle the local gov'ment as well as I handle other things, and he'll do all that's necessary. What he'd ought to attend to, for one thing, is this here guy who calls himself the Midnight Masquer. I've told him before that this guy was playing hell with my system! This Masquer gets no protection, see? The quicker Fell goes after him, the better for all concerned——"

Chacherre laughed, not without a swagger.

"We've attended to all that, Izzy—we've dropped on him and settled him! The guy was doin' it for a carnival joke, that's all. His loot is all goin' back to the owners to-day. It needn't worry you, anyhow! There was nothin' much to it—jewellery that couldn't be disposed of, for the most part. We couldn't take chances on that sort o' junk."

"I should say not." Gumbert regarded him with a scowl. "You've got the stuff?"

"The boss has. Look here, Izzy, I want you to use a little influence with headquarters on this deal—the boss doesn't want to show his hand there," and leaning forward, Ben Chacherre spoke in a low tone. Then, Gumberts heard him out, chuckled, and nodded assent.

At two that afternoon Henry Gramont, who was writing letters in total disregard of the carnival parade downtown, was summoned to the telephone. He was greeted by a voice which he did not recognize, but which announced itself promptly.

"This is Mr. Gramont? Police headquarters speakin'. You laid a charge this morning against a fellow named Chacherre?"

"Yes," answered Gramont.

"Must ha' been some mistake, then," came the response. "We thought the prints fitted, but found later they didn't. We looked up the Chacherre guy and found he was workin' steady and strictly O. K. What's more to the point, he proved up a dead sure alibi for the other night."

"Oh!" said Gramont. "Then there's nothing to be done?"

"Not yet. We're workin' on it, and maybe we'll have some news later. Good-bye."

Gramont hung up the receiver, a puzzled frown creasing his brow. But, after a minute, he laughed softly—a trace of anger in the laugh.

"Ah!" he murmured. "I congratulate you on your efficiency, Mr. Fell! But now wait a little—and we'll meet again. I think I'm getting somewhere at last, and I'll have a surprise for you one of these days!"

CHAPTER 7: IN THE OPEN

In New Orleans the carnival season is always opened by the ball of the Twelfth Night Revellers soon after Christmas, and is closed by that of the Krewe of Comus on Mardi Gras night. Upon this evening of "Fat Tuesday," indeed, both Rex and Comus hold forth. Rex is the popular ball, the affair of the people, and is held in the Athenaeum. From here, about midnight, the king and queen proceed to Comus ball.

Comus is an assembly of such rigid exclusiveness that even the tickets to the galleries are considered social prizes. The *personae* of the Krewe, on this particular year as in all previous ones, would remain unknown; there is no unmasking at Comus. This institution, a tremendous social power and potentially a financial power also, during decades of the city's life, is held absolutely above any taint of favouritism or commercialism. Even the families of those concerned might not always be certain whether their sons and brothers belonged to the Krewe of Comus.

Henry Gramont did not attend the ball of Proteus on Monday night. Instead, he sat in his own room, while through the streets of the French quarter outside was raging the carnival at its height. Before him were maps and reports upon the gas and oil fields about Bayou Terrebonne—fields where great domes of natural gas were already located and in use, and where oil was being found in some quantity. Early on Wednesday morning Gramont intended to set forth to his work. He had been engaged to make a report to Bob Maillard's company, and he would make it. Then he would resign his advisory job, and be free. A smile curled his lips as he thought of young Maillard and the company.

"The young gentleman will be sadly surprised to discover that I've gotten out from under—and that his respected father holds my stock!" he reflected. "That was a good deal; I lost a thousand to old Maillard in order to save the balance of thirty thousand!"

A knock at his door interrupted the thread of this thought. Gramont opened, to find the concierge with a note which had been left at the door below by a masked Harlequin, who had then disappeared without awaiting any reply.

Gramont recognized the writing on the envelope, and hastened to the note inside. His face changed, however, as he read it:

Please call promptly at eleven to-morrow morning. I wish to see you upon a matter of business.
LUCIE LEDANOIS.

Gramont gazed long at this note, his brows drawn down into a harsh line. It was not like Lucie in its tone, somehow; he sensed something amiss, something vaguely but most decidedly out of tune. Certainly it was not her way to write thus curtly and harshly—the words disquieted him. What could have turned up now? Then, with a shrug, he tossed the note on the table.

"Eleven to-morrow morning, eh?" he murmured. "That's queer, too, for she's to be at the Proteus ball to-night. Most girls would not be conducting business affairs at eleven in the morning, after being up all night at Proteus! It must be something important. Besides, she's not in the class with any one else. She's a rare girl; no nonsense in her—full of a deep, strong sense of things——"

He forced himself from thoughts of Lucie, forced himself from her personality, and returned to his reports with an effort of concentration.

Gramont wanted to look over her Terrebonne land with a full knowledge of its geology and situation. Oil drilling is a gamble in any case, yet Gramont took a scholar's solid satisfaction in getting his subject thoroughly in hand before he went to work at it. Then, he reflected, he would get his task finished as rapidly as might be, turn in his report, and resign from the company. After that—freedom! He regretted sadly enough that he had ever gone into any relations with Maillard's company.

"Yet, what's to hinder my going ahead, in the meantime?" he considered. "What's to hinder getting my own company on its feet? Nothing! All I need is backing. I'll put in twenty-five thousand, and that much more added to it will give us plenty of capital to start in drilling with. If I could find someone who had a positive faith in my judgment and whom I could trust in turn——"

He checked himself suddenly, and stared at the papers before him with widening eyes. A slow whistle came from his lips, and then he smiled and pulled the papers to him. Yet, as he worked he could not keep down the thought that had forced itself upon him. It was altogether absurd, of course—yet why not?

When Gramont went to bed that night it was with a startling and audacious scheme well defined in his brain; a scheme whose first conception seemed ludicrous and impossible, yet which, on second consideration, appeared in a very different light. It deserved serious thought—and Gramont had made his decision before he went to sleep.

The following day was Tuesday—Mardi Gras, Shrove Tuesday, the last day before Lent began, and the final culminating day of carnival. Henry Gramont, however, was destined to find little in its beginning of much personal pleasure.

At eleven in the morning Hammond drove him to the Ledanois home, where Gramont was admitted by one of the coloured servants and shown into the parlour. A moment later Lucie herself appeared. At first glance her smiling greeting removed the half-sensed apprehensions of Gramont. Almost immediately afterward, however, he noted a perceptible change in her manner, as she led him toward the rear of the room, and gestured toward a mahogany tilt-top table which stood in a corner.

"Come over here, please. I have something which I wish to show you."

She needed to say no more. Gramont, following her, found himself staring blankly down at the symbol of consternation which overwhelmed him. For upon that table, lay all those self-same boxes which he himself had packed with the loot of the Midnight Masquer—the identical boxes, apparently unopened, which had been stolen from his automobile by the supposed thief Chacherre!

For a moment Gramont found himself unable to speak. He was thunderstruck by the sight of those unmistakeable boxes. A glance at the calm features of the girl showed him that there was nothing to be concealed from her, even had he wished it. He was further stunned by this realization. He could not understand how the packages had come here. Recovering his voice with an effort, he managed to break the heavy silence.

"Well? I suppose you know what is in those parcels?"

She nodded. "Yes. One of them was opened, and the note inside was discovered. Of course, it gave a general explanation. Will you sit down, please? I think that we had better talk it over quietly and calmly."

Gramont obeyed, and dropped into a chair.

He was absurdly conscious of his own confusion. He tried to speak, but words and thoughts failed him. Torn between pride and chagrin, he found himself able to say nothing. Explanations, at any time, came to him with difficulty; now, at least, he felt that he could not lie to this girl. And how was he to tell her the truth?

And how had Lucie come into the affair? This staggered him above all else. Was she behind the theft of the loot? It must be. How long had she suspected him, then? He had thought Jachin Fell the sole danger-point— he had never dreamed that this gray-eyed Athene could be tracing down the Masquer! He tried to visualize the situation more clearly and his brain whirled. He knew, of course, that she was fairly intimate with Fell, but he was not aware of any particular connection——

He glanced up at her suddenly, and surprised a glint of laughter in her eyes as she watched him.

"You seem to be rather astonished," she observed.

"I am." Gramont drew a deep breath. "You—do you know that those boxes were taken from my car?"

She nodded again. "Certainly. They were brought to me."

"Then you had someone on my trail?" Gramont flushed a little as he put the question to her.

"No. I have been chosen to settle affairs with you, that is all. It has been learned from the note in the opened box that you were not criminal in what you did."

She leaned forward, her deep eyes searching him with a steady scrutiny.

"Tell me, Henry Gramont, what mad impulse brought you to all this? Was it a silly, boyish effort to be romantic—was it a mere outburst of bravado? It was not for the sake of robbery, as the note explained very clearly. But why, then? Why? There must have been a definite reason in your mind. You would not have taken such dangerous chances unless you had something to gain!"

Gramont nodded slightly, then flushed again and bit his lip. For a moment he made no response to her query.

He might, of course, say that he had been the Midnight Masquer because of her alone; which would be decidedly untrue. He might tell her, as he had told Hammond, that all his efforts had led up to that scene in the Maillard library, when without suspicion by any concerned he might verify his own surmise as to who had been defrauding Lucie Ledanois. It would sound very well—but it would be a lie. That had been far from his only reason for playing the Midnight Masquer's game.

But why tell her anything?

A slight smile touched his lips. "You're not going to send me to prison, I trust?"

"I ought to!" The girl broke into a laugh. "Why, I can hardly yet believe that it was really you who were guilty of those things! It mortified me, it stunned me—until I realized the truth from the note. Even the fact that you did not do it for criminal ends does not relieve the sheer folly of the act. Why did you do it? Come, tell me the truth!"

Gramont shrugged. "The truth? Well, my chauffeur, Hammond, was the original Masquer. I caught him in the act—you remember I told you about him? After taking him into my employ, I became the Masquer. Poor Hammond was some time in realizing that my motives were altruistic and not criminal. He was quite distressed about it until he found that I meant to return all the loot intact."

"Why did you do it, then?" persisted the girl.

"Call it bravado, my dear Lucie. Call it anything you like—I can't lie to you! I had a motive, and I refuse to admit what it was; that's all."

"Aren't you ashamed of yourself?"

"Not particularly." He smiled. "I had a good end in view, and I accomplished it. Also, I flatter myself that I accomplished it very decently; there's nothing like being a good workman, you know. Now that I'm all through, now that I've finished playing my little game, you happened to discover it. I am ashamed on that point, Lucie—ashamed because the discovery has very naturally made you think harshly of me——"

"I think you've been very silly," she said with a disconcerting calmness. He regarded her for a moment, steadily. "And you have displayed a fearful lack of judgment!"

"Silly? Well—perhaps. What are you going to do with those boxes?"

"I'll put them in the mail. I'm going downtown for luncheon, and will do it then. They'll be delivered this afternoon."

He nodded. "I had meant to have them delivered to-morrow; it makes no difference. You're the boss. It will give the good people a little more reason for jubilation to-night, eh?"

A sudden laugh broke upon his lips. "I'm beginning to see the humour of it, Lucie—and I know who put you next to me. It was Jachin Fell, the old fox! I suspected that he was on my trail, and I thought that he had managed the theft of those boxes. In fact, I was preparing to give him a big surprise this afternoon. But tell me, Lucie—are you angry?"

She looked at him steadily for a space, then a swift smile leaped to her lips and she extended a pardoning hand. Her gesture and words were impulsive, sincere.

"Angry? No. I think you've some good reason behind it all, which you won't confide to me. I can read you pretty clearly, Henry Gramont; I think I can understand some things in you. You're no weakling, no romantic, filibustering crackbrain! And I like you because you won't lie to me. You've a motive and you refuse to tell it—very well! I'll be just as frank and say that I'm not a bit angry. So, that's settled!

"Now what was the big surprise that you just mentioned you were going to give poor Mr. Fell this afternoon?"

Gramont's eyes twinkled. "You remember that I thought he suspected me of being the Masquer? Well, I was going to him and propose that we enter business together."

"Oh! As bandits?"

"No, as oil promotors. I'm out of Maillard's company, or shall be out of it soon. The minute I'm out, I'll be free to go into business for myself. It occurred to me that if Jachin Fell had brains enough to run down the Midnight Masquer, he would be a mighty good business partner;

because I'm poor on business detail. Also, I think Fell is to be trusted. The things you've told me and written me about him prove that much. He's very strong politically, I have found—although few people know it."

"But he's not interested in oil is he?"

"I don't know; I take for granted that he's interested in making money. Most men are. The only way to make money in oil is to have money—and he has some! I have a little. I can put in twenty-five thousand. With an equal amount from him, we can sink a couple of wells, perhaps three. If we go broke, all right. If we find oil, we're rich!"

"But, my dear Henry, if he knew you to be the Midnight Masquer, do you think he'd want to go into business with you?" Her gray eyes were dancing with amusement as she put the query.

"Why not?" Gramont laughed. "If he knew that I had brains enough to pull off that stunt and keep all New Orleans up in the air—wouldn't I make a good partner? Besides, I believe that I have some notion where to go after oil; I'm going to examine your land first——"

"My good prince, you surely have no lack of audacity!" She broke into a peal of laughter. "Your argument about inducing Mr. Fell to go into business with you is naive——"

"But, as an argument, isn't it quite sound?"

"Possibly. Since it is Lucie Ledanois and not Jachin Fell who has brought you to a confession of your crimes against society—aren't you going to propose that she go into business with you? Doesn't the argument hold good with her?"

Although Gramont was taken aback, he met her gaze squarely.

"No. Oil is no woman's game, unless she can well afford to lose. I imagine that you cannot, Lucie. Once I get my company formed, however——"

"You're right, I can't put in any money. I'm land poor. Unless I were to sell that Bayou Terrebonne land—it's an old farm, abandoned since before father died——"

"Don't sell it!" he exclaimed, quickly. "Don't consider any dealings with it until I have looked it over, will you?"

"Since you ask it, no. If there's gas near by, there must be oil."

"Who knows?" he shrugged. "No one can predict oil."

"Then you still mean to go to Jachin Fell with your scheme?"

Gramont nodded. "Yes. See here, Lucie—it's about noon! Suppose you come along and lunch with me at the Louisiane, if you've no engagement. We can put those boxes in the mail en route, and after luncheon I'll try and get hold of Fell."

She put her head on one side and studied him reflectively.

"You're sure you'll not kidnap me or anything like that? It's risky to become a friend of hardened criminals, even if one is trying to uplift them."

"Good! You'll come?"

"If you can give me ten minutes——"

"My dear Lucie, you are the most charming object in New Orleans at this minute! Why attempt to make yourself still more attractive? Gilding the lily is an impossible task."

"Well, wait for me. Is your car here? Good! I want to see Hammond's face when he sees us carrying out those boxes."

Laughing, the girl started toward the stairs. At the doorway she paused.

"One thing, M. le prince! Do you solemnly promise, upon your honour, that the Midnight Masquer is dead for ever?"

"Upon my honour!" said Gramont, seriously. "The farce is ended, Lucie."

"All right. I'll be right down. Smoke if you like——"

In her own room upstairs Lucie closed the door and sat down before her dressing table. She made no move toward the array of toilet articles, however. Instead, she took a desk telephone from the table, and called a number. In a moment she received a response.

"Uncle Jachin!" she exclaimed. "Yes—it's just as we thought; it's all a joke. No, it was not a joke, either, because he had some motive behind it, but he won't tell me what it was. I'm terribly glad that you opened one of those boxes and found the letter—if you had gone to the police it would have been perfectly dreadful——"

"I never go to the police," said Jachin Fell with his dry chuckle. "You are quite satisfied that there is nothing serious in the affair, then?"

"Absolutely! He told me that he had accomplished his purpose, whatever it was, and that it's all ended. He just gave me his word that the Masquer was dead for ever. Now, aren't you glad that you confided in me?"

"Very," said Jachin Fell. "Very glad, indeed!"

"Now you're laughing at me—never mind! We're going to lunch downtown, and we'll mail those boxes on the way, by parcels post. Is that all right?"

"Quite all right, my dear. It is the method adopted by the most exclusive and elusive criminals in the country, I assure you. Every handbag snatcher gets rid of his empty bags by mailing them back to the owner—unless first caught. It pays to follow professional examples, as Eliza said when she crossed the ice. Did your gown come for to-night?"

"It's to come this afternoon."

"Very well. Do not plan to wear any jewels, Lucie. I have a set to lend you for the occasion—no, not a gift, merely a loan for the sake of Comus. They are very nice pearls; a little old fashioned, because they were mounted for the Princesses de Lamballe, but you will find that they fit in excellently with your gown. I'll bring them with me when I call for you——"

"And I'll tender fitting thanks then. One thing more: Henry Gramont is going to see you after luncheon, I think—on business. And I want you to be nice to him, Uncle Jachin."

"Most assuredly," said the other, drily. "I should like to be associated in business with that young man. The firm would prosper."

"Will you stop laughing at me? Then I'll ring off—good-bye!"

And, smiling, she hung up the receiver.

Ten minutes later, when Gramont and Miss Ledanois entered the waiting car, Hammond saw the boxes that they carried. He stood beside the open door, paralyzed, his eyes fastened on the boxes, his mouth agape.

"To the postoffice, sergeant," said Gramont, then affected to observe his stupefaction. "Why, what's the matter?"

Hammond met his twinkling eyes, saw the laughter of Lucie, and swallowed hard.

"I—er—nothing at all, cap'n," he answered, hoarsely. "A—a little chokin' spell, that's all. Postoffice? Yes, sir."

CHAPTER 8: COMUS

From the time they left the Ledanois house with Lucie, Gramont had no opportunity of seeing his chauffeur in private until, later in the afternoon, he left the Maison Blanche building. He had enjoyed a thoroughly satisfactory interview with Jachin Fell. So wholly had Gramont's thoughts been given over to the business, indeed, that it was almost a shock to emerge into Canal Street and find everyone else in the world thinking only of the water carnival and the Rex parade.

As for the Midnight Masquer and the mystery of the boxes of loot, all this had quite fled Gramont's mind before larger and more important things. The car was waiting for him in Royal Street, not far from the Monteleone, and Gramont approached it to find Hammond in deep worry over the outcome of the interview with Fell.

"Well, cap'n!" he exclaimed, anxiously, as Gramont drew up. "You're smilin', so I guess it ain't a pinch!"

Gramont laughed gaily. "Those boxes? Nonsense! Say, sergeant, you must have been scared stiff when you saw them!"

"Scared? I was ready to flop, that's all! And how in the name o' goodness did they get in *her* house? What's behind all this?"

Gramont glanced around. He walked with Hammond to the front of the car, where he could speak without being overheard by the passersby.

"It seems that I was more or less mistaken about Fell being on our trail," he explained, reflectively. "We had a very frank talk about it, and he disclaimed all knowledge of the boxes themselves. I gathered from little things he dropped that some criminal had looted the stuff from the car, and that it came to his attention yesterday in a legal capacity——"

"Legal capacity, hell!" snorted Hammond. "Did you swallow all that?"

"My swallowing capacity was pretty good," and Gramont chuckled. "It seems that he opened one of the boxes, and found the note I had written. This explained the business, and by way of a little joke he turned over the loot to Miss Ledanois and she had a bit of fun with us. Fell, in fact, proved to be a pretty good fellow——"

"He sure handed you out a fine line of bull!" commented Hammond, savagely. "What gets me is your falling for all that dope! Looks like you wanted to believe him, cap'n."

"Perhaps I did." Gramont shrugged his shoulders. "Why not? I've no reason to disbelieve him. The note made it plain that we were not criminals; now the whole affair is cleaned up and out of the way. We're out of it in good shape, if you ask me!"

"You said something there," agreed Hammond, not without a sigh of relief. "All right, if you say so, only I ain't sure about this Fell——"

"Don't worry. The stuff is returned, and the matter is now closed. We can forget all about the Midnight Masquer. Now, there's another and more important thing that I want to speak with you about, a matter of business——"

"Hold on, cap'n!" interrupted Hammond, quietly, his eye on a spot behind Gramont. "One of your friends is headed over this way, and if I know anything about it, he's got blood in his eye."

Gramont turned, to see Bob Maillard approaching. The latter addressed him without any response to his greeting.

"Have you a moment to spare, Gramont?"

"All afternoon," answered Gramont, cheerfully. He affected not to observe Maillard's air of heavy business, nor the frowning suspicion that lurked half-veiled in the other's glowering features. "By the way, I've been looking up a New Orleans landmark without much success—the Ramos gin fizz establishment. It seems to be gone!"

"It is," returned Maillard, sourly. "Prohibition killed it, like it's killing everything. Francois moved into the place last September from Old 27, and it's become his restaurant now. But look here, Gramont!" The two were standing a bit apart, and Hammond was fussing with one of the headlights, but Gramont suspected that the chauffeur was listening avidly. "I've just come from a talk with dad. How did it happen that you sold him that stock of yours in the company?"

Gramont smiled a little. He was amused by the way Maillard was endeavouring to keep down an outburst of angry passion.

"I happened to need the money. Why?"

"But why the devil didn't you hang on to that stock? Or if you needed money, why didn't you come to me?" exploded the other, angrily.

"Heavens!" drawled Gramont, who was quite willing to exasperate young Maillard to the limit. "You seem frightfully concerned about it! What's the big idea, anyway? I don't recall that any of us went into an agreement not to sell if we wanted to. I offered the stock to your father at a discount. He realized that it was a good buy, and took it. What's wrong with that?"

"Nothing wrong, if you put it that way," snapped Maillard, angrily. "But it's a confounded sly way of doing things——"

"Now, just wait right there!" Gramont's easy smile vanished. "I don't take that kind of talk, Maillard. One more such insinuation, and you'll need to use a mask at the ball to-night, I promise you! I'll show you how sly I am, my friend! I'm off in the morning to start work on that report I was engaged to make. When the report comes in, my resignation comes with it."

"All right. Let it come here and now, then." Maillard's tone was ugly. "If you're so blamed anxious to get out of the company, get out!"

"Thanks. I'll be glad to be relieved of the job." Gramont turned and addressed his chauffeur. "Hammond, you'll kindly remember this conversation, in case your future testimony is needed——"

"Confound you, what d'you mean talking that way?" broke out Maillard. "Do you suppose I'll deny firing you?"

"I don't care to have you offer any reflections on my actions, Maillard," said Gramont, evenly. "My course in this matter is perfectly open and above board, which is more than you can say for your doings."

"What?" Maillard clenched his stick and took a forward step, anger working in his face. "What the devil d'you mean?"

"Exactly what I say—and perhaps I can prove it. Remember the oil concern to which you persuaded your precious father to sell some of Miss Ledanois's bayou land? Remember the real estate company to which you persuaded him to sell her St. Landry parish property? You had interests in both concerns; I don't imagine you'd care to have your share in those transactions exposed. Further, I entirely understand your indignation over my getting rid of this stock before the crash, and it ill becomes you to assume any such attitude."

Maillard glared at him for a long moment, a red tide of rage flooding and ebbing from his heavy countenance. Then, mastering himself, he turned and strode away without further speech.

"Hurray!" observed Hammond, when he was gone. "Cap'n, that guy is off you for life! I bet he'd like to meet you alone on a dark night!"

Gramont shook his head. "He's a bad enemy, all right. Here, get into the car!"

He climbed in beside Hammond.

"Don't drive—I want to speak with you. Now that Maillard has relieved me of the necessity of making any report to his company, I'm free, and glad of it! I've been talking business with Mr. Fell, and I'm to have my own company."

"With him?" Hammond sniffed.

"Yes. He's matching his money against mine, and we're going to look for oil on some land owned by Miss Ledanois. It'll be a close corporation, and if we strike oil, we'll all three have a good thing. We may go broke, and we may go rich; if you're saving any coin out of your salary and feel like taking a gamble, I'll get you a bit of the stock after Mr. Fell gets things in shape. You can think it over——"

"I don't want to think it over," broke in Hammond, eagerly. "I'm on, here and now—and it sure is mighty good of you, cap'n! Say, I ain't had any chance to tell you before, but I pulled two hundred out o' the lottery last week——"

"Lottery!" Gramont looked at him quickly. "What lottery?"

Hammond looked a trifle sheepish. "Well, it's against the law, o' course, but they run 'em right along just the same. A bunch of the chauffeurs here are wise to it; they put up some coin for me last week, and as I was sayin' I pulled out two hundred. I got most of it left, and have some saved up on the side. I'll stick it all in, huh?"

Gramont nodded. "Well, we'll see later. You're free until morning, sergeant. I'm going to the Comus ball to-night as a guest of the Lavergnes, and they'll call for me. Enjoy yourself, keep out of jail, and be ready to start at six in the morning for Terrebonne."

Leaving Hammond to take the car home, Gramont headed for Canal Street to mingle with the carnival crowd and revel in his new-found sense of freedom. Now that he was his own master, he felt like a new man.

Overnight, it seemed, all weights had dropped from his shoulders. On the score of the Midnight Masquer, he was vastly relieved; all that was over and forgotten. Financially, he had achieved what was nothing less than a masterly triumph. In a business way, he was free of all ties and able to look forward to decisive action on his own behalf and that of a partner in whom he could feel a perfect reliance.

Consequently, he began really to enjoy Mardi Gras for the first time, and plunged into the eddying crowds in a free and light-hearted manner which had not been his for years.

It was the moment for the carnival spirit to seize on him, and seize him it did. With a boyish abandon he tramped the streets merrily, exchanging jests and confetti, shoves and bladder-blows, laughs and kisses. Madness and reckless gaiety were in the very air, and Gramont drank deep of these youthful tonics. When at last he wandered home to his pension, he was footsore, weary, disarranged, and touseled—and very happy. The wine of human comradeship is a good wine.

That evening the Comus ball, the most exclusive revel of the most exclusive aristocracy of the southland, crowded the edifice in which it was held to capacity. Here evening dress was prescribed for all the guests. The Krewe of Comus alone were masked and costumed, in grotesque and magnificent costumes which had been in the making for months. The Krewe is to the South what the Bohemian Club is to the western coast, with the added enhancement of mystery.

Despite the revels of the Krewe, however—despite the glittering jewels, the barbaric costumes, the music, the excitement—an indefinable air of regret, almost of sadness, pervaded the entire gathering. This feeling was something to be sensed, rather than observed definitely. Some said, afterward, that it was a premonition of the terrible event that was to happen this night. Wrong! It was because, for the first time in many generations, the Comus ball was held in one of the newer public buildings instead of in its accustomed place. Everyone was speaking of it. Even Maillard the banker, that cold man of dollars, spoke uneasily of it when Gramont encountered him in the smoking room.

"It doesn't seem like Comus," said Maillard, with a vexed frown. "And to think that we had just finished redecorating the Opera House when it was burned down! Comus will never be the same again."

"I didn't know you could feel such emotion for a ruined building, Maillard," said Gramont, lightly. The banker shrugged a trifle.

"Emotion? No. Regret! None of us, who has been brought up in the traditions of the city but regarded the French Opera House as the centre of all our storied life. You can't understand it, Gramont; no outsider can. By the way, you haven't seen Bob? He's in costume, but he might have spoken to you——"

Gramont answered in the negative, with a slight surprise at the question.

It was not long before he came to comprehend more fully just what the loss of the old French Opera House meant to the assembly. He heard comparisons made on every hand, regretful allusions, sighs for the days that were no more.

This present building, to be sure, was one of the city's finest, up to date in every way, with an abundance of room—and yet everyone said that Comus would never be the same. About the Opera House had clung the romance of many generations. About it, too, had clung the affections of the people with a fierceness beyond reason. More famous buildings had been allowed to go to ruin, like the Hotel Royale, but the Opera House had been kept in repair for Mardi Gras. It was itself—a landmark. Nothing else would ever be like it.

From his seat in the Lavergne box Gramont contented himself during the early evening with the common role of all the "blackcoats"—that of looking on idly. More than once he saw Lucie Ledanois called out, among others of the fair sex, as a dancing partner for some member of the Krewe. None of the male guests, however, was allowed to participate in the festivity until Rex and his queen should arrive—at midnight; thus, Gramont saw almost nothing of Lucie during the evening.

There was, inevitably, more or less visiting in boxes and foyers, and not a little lounging in the smoking room. The building was a huge structure, and richly furnished. Only a portion of it was in use by the Krewe; the remainder was, of course, deserted for the time being.

While in search of smoking companions, Gramont encountered many of his acquaintances, and among them Doctor Ansley and Jachin Fell. In order to enjoy Fell's proffered El Reys in a somewhat clearer atmosphere these three strolled off together into one of the unused passages leading to other parts of the building. They opened a window and stood watching the crowd that surged in the street below, constantly increasing as the hour grew later, for the procession of Rex would be well worth seeing and nobody meant to miss anything upon this night of nights.

Suddenly, at the sound of an approaching footstep, the three men turned. The electric lights were going in all of the hallways, and they perceived that the individual approaching them was a member of the Krewe of Comus. He was also, it became evident, giving a share of his allegiance to Bacchus, for his feet were obviously unsteady. He was clad in a parti-coloured costume, which was crowned by an exaggerated head of Mephisto.

"Good evening to you, worthy gentlemen!" He came to a fuddled halt and stood there, laughing at the stares of the three. "Evening, I say."

They responded to his liquor-tinged words with a laughing reply.

"Wonderin' who I am, aren't you!" he hiccuped. "Well, don't wonder; 'sall between ol' friends to-night! Tell you what, m' friends—come with me and I'll find you a li'l drink, eh? No prohibition booze, upon m' honour; real old Boone pinchneck—got it from some boys in Louisville, been savin' it up for to-night."

He wagged his head at them, and pursued his subject in a half-maudlin burst of confidential assurance. An unsteady hand waved down the hallway.

"Havin' a little party in one of the rooms," he continued. "All of us friends—lots more fun than dancin'! And say! I'm going pull something great, positively great; you don't want to miss it, gentlemen! You come along with me and I'll fix it for you. Come on, Gramont, that's a good fellow! You'n I had a dis'greement to-day—don't matter to-night, nothin' matters to-night, nothin' at all. Mardi Gras only comes once a year, eh? Come along, now."

Jachin Fell very civilly refused the invitation, as did the others. Gramont, who now recognized their accoster, was less civil in his refusal. Mephisto sadly wagged his huge headpiece and regarded them with vinous regret.

"No 'joyment in you any more? Better come along. Tell you, I've got the biggest joke of the season ready to pull off—something rich! Gramont, come on!"

"Thanks, no," responded Gramont, curtly.

The masquer gave up the struggle and moved on down the empty hallway. The three "blackcoats" watched in silence until the grotesque figure had vanished.

"I wonder who that was, now?" mused Doctor Ansley, frowning. "Evidently, someone who knew us; at least, he recognized you, Gramont."

"So it seemed," put in Jachin Fell. His tone, like his eyes, held a sombre fire. "A party of them drinking, eh? that will make trouble. The Krewe won't like it. Ten to one, that young man and his friends will start the makings of a fine scandal and the Krewe will come down hard on them—mighty hard. Who was he, Gramont? Sounded like——"

"Young Maillard." At Gramont's response a whistle broke from Doctor Ansley. Jachin Fell nodded assent.

"You took the words out of my mouth. So Bob is drinking again, eh? And they've occupied one of the rooms somewhere, and are enjoying a bit of liquor and a card game by themselves. Cursed slippery going, as Eliza said when she crossed the ice! The Krewe will expel them. Hello, Gramont—where to?"

Gramont tossed his cigar through the open window.

"I think I'll make my adieux, Fell. I intend to be up early in the morning and get off to work——"

"What?" protested Ansley in astonishment. "You must stay until Rex comes, at least! Why, that's the event of the carnival! The evening hasn't started yet."

"I'm growing old and sober, doctor," and Gramont chuckled. "To tell the truth," and he gave Fell a whimsical glance, "I am head over ears in some new business matters which have actually fired me with the divine afflatus of enthusiasm. What's more, I was drifting with the crowds all afternoon, and I've just begun to realize that I'm dead tired. Rex or no Rex, I'm afraid that I'd best say good-night, gentlemen."

Gramont persisted in his intention, and bade the other two good-night. In truth, he cared very little about Rex, and a very great deal about getting off to Bayou Terrebonne early in the morning. The oil matter filled his mind. He had formed a thousand plans, he was fired with enthusiasm, and was anxious to make his preliminary investigation.

Returning to the auditorium, Gramont sought out his hosts and made his farewells, although not without encountering some opposition. At length he was free, he had obtained his hat and coat, and as he passed out of the building he again met Fell and Ansley, who were finishing their cigars at the entrance. He bade them a final adieu and plunged into the crowd.

It lacked half an hour of midnight. The streets were filled with merrymakers, who were making the night riotous with songs, yells, and noise-producing apparatus, anticipating the arrival of Rex. For a little Fell and Doctor Ansley stood talking, then tossed away their cigars and turned into the building.

They halted in the foyer before the appearance of two men—Joseph Maillard, looking extremely agitated, and behind him old Judge Forester, who wore a distinctly worried expression.

"Ah, here are Fell and Ansley!" exclaimed Maillard, almost with relief. "I—ah—my friends, I don't suppose you've seen Bob recently?"

Ansley was silent. Jachin Fell, however, responded with a cold nod of assent.

"Yes," he said in his peculiarly toneless manner. "Yes, we have. At least, I believe it was he——"

"I'm worried," said Maillard, anxiously, hurriedly. He made an expressive gesture of despair. "He's in costume, of course. I've been given to understand that—well, that he has been—well, drinking."

"He has," said Jachin Fell, without any trace of compassion. "A number of the Krewe are occupying one of the rooms in the building, and they must have been visiting it frequently. I trust for your sake that the fact hasn't become generally known inside?"

Maillard nodded. Shame and anger lay heavily in his eyes.

"Yes, Jachin. I—I was asked to exert my influence over Bob. The request came to me from the floor. This—this is a disgraceful thing to admit, my friends——"

Judge Forester, in his kindly way, laid his hand on the banker's arm.

"Tut, tut, Joseph," he said, gently, a fund of sympathy in his voice. "Boys will be boys, you know; really, this is no great matter! Don't let it hit you so hard. I'll go with you to find the room, of course. Where is it, Jachin?"

"We'll all go," put in Ansley. "We'll have a little party of our own, gentlemen. Come on, I believe we'll be able to discover the place."

The four men left the foyer and started through the corridors. Among them was a tacit understanding, a deep feeling of sympathy for Joseph Maillard, a bond which held them to his aid in this disgrace which had befallen him. Jachin Fell, who felt the least compassion or pity, cursed Bob Maillard—but under his breath.

They walked through the empty, lighted corridors, following the direction in which Fell and Ansley had seen young Maillard disappear.

"I hear," said Judge Forester to Doctor Ansley, as they followed the other two, "that there has been astonishing news to-day from the Midnight Masquer. It seems that a number of people have received back property this afternoon—loot the bandit had taken. It came by mail, special delivery. One of the Lavergne boys tells me that they received a box containing everything that was taken at their home, even to cash, with a note asking them to return the things to their guests. It appears to have been some sort of a carnival joke, after all."

"A poor one, then," responded Ansley, "and in doubtful taste. I've heard nothing of it. I wouldn't mind getting back the little cash I lost, though I must say I'll believe the story when I see the money——"

He broke off quickly.

As they turned a corner of the corridor to the four men came realization that they had attained their goal. From one of the rooms ahead there sounded snatches of a boisterous chorus being roared forth lustily. As they halted, to distinguish from which door the singing proceeded, the chorus was broken off by an abrupt and sudden silence. This silence was accentuated by the preceding noise, as though the singers had checked their maudlin song in mid-career.

"Damn it!" muttered Maillard. "Did they hear us coming? No, that wouldn't matter a hang to them—but what checked them so quickly?"

"This door," said Fell, indicating one to their right. He paused at it, listening, and over his features came a singular expression. As the others joined him, they caught a low murmur of voices, a hushed sound of talk, a rattle as a number of chips fell from a table.

"Cursed queer!" observed Jachin Fell, frowning. "I wonder what happened to them so abruptly? Perhaps the deal was finished—they're having a game. Well, go ahead, Joseph! We'll back you up as a deputation from the blackcoats, and if you need any moral support, call on Judge Forester."

"Correct!" assented that gentleman with dignity. "I'll give these jackanapes a little advice! It's going a bit far, this sort of thing; we can't have Comus turned into a common drinking bout. Ready, Joseph?"

He flung open the door, and Maillard entered at his side. They then came to a startled halt, at view of the scene which greeted them.

The room was large and well lighted, windows and transom darkened for the occasion. Tobacco smoke made a bluish haze in the air. In the centre of the room stood a large table, littered with glasses and bottles, with scattered cards, with chips and money.

About this table had been sitting half a dozen members of the Krewe of Comus. Now, however, they were standing, their various identities completely concealed by the grotesque costumes which cloaked them. Their hands were in the air.

Standing at another doorway, midway between their group and that of the four unexpected intruders, was the Midnight Masquer—holding them up at the point of his automatic!

There was a moment of tense and strained silence, as every eye went to the four men in evening attire. It was plain what had cut short the boisterous song—the Masquer must have made his appearance only a moment or two previously. From head to foot he was hidden under his leathern attire. His unrecognizable features, at this instant, were turned slightly toward the four new arrivals. It was obvious that he, no less than the others, was startled by this entry.

Maillard was the first to break that silence of stupefaction.

"By heavens!" he cried, furiously. "Here's that damned villain again—hold him, you! at him, everybody!"

In a blind rage, transported out of himself by his sudden access of passion, the banker hurled himself forward. From the bandit burst a cry of futile warning; the pistol in his hand veered toward his assailant.

This action precipitated the event. Perhaps because the Masquer did not fire instantly, and perhaps because Maillard's mad action shamed them, the nearer members of the drinking party hurled themselves at the bandit. The threat of the weapon was forgotten, unheeded in the sweeping lust of the man-hunt. It seemed that the fellow feared to fire; and about him closed the party in a surging mass, with a burst of sudden shouts, striking and clutching to pull him down and put him under foot.

Then, when it seemed that they had him without a struggle, the Masquer broke from them, swept them apart and threw them off, hurled them clear away. He moved as though to leap through the side doorway whence he had come.

With an oath, Maillard hurled himself forward, struck blindly and furiously at the bandit, and fastened upon him about the waist. There was a surge forward of bodies as the others crowded in to pull down the Masquer before he could escape. It looked then as though he were indeed lost—until the automatic flamed and roared in his hand, its choking fumes bursting at them. The report thundered in the room; a second report thundered, deafeningly, as a second bullet sought its mark.

Like a faint echo to those shots came the slam of a door. The Masquer was gone!

After him, into the farther room, rushed some of the party; but he had vanished utterly. There was no trace of him. Of course, he might have ducked into any of the dark rooms, or have run down the corridor, yet his complete disappearance confused the searchers. After a moment, however, they returned to the lighted room. The

Masquer had gone, but behind him had remained a more grim and terrible masquer.

In the room which he had just left, however, there had fallen a dread silence and consternation. One of the masqued drinkers held an arm that hung helpless, dripping blood; but his hurt passed unseen and uncared for, even by himself.

Doctor Ansley was kneeling above a motionless figure, prone on the dirty floor; and it was the figure of Joseph Maillard. The physician glanced up, then rose slowly to his feet. He made a terribly significant gesture, and his crisp voice broke in upon the appalled silence.

"Dead," he said, curtly. "Shot twice—each bullet through the heart. Judge Forester, I'm afraid there is no alternative but to call in the police. Gentlemen, you will kindly unmask—which one of you is Robert Maillard?"

Amid a stunned and horrified silence the members of the Krewe one by one removed their grotesque headgear, staring at the dead man whose white face looked up at them with an air of grim accusation. But none of them came forward to claim kinship with the dead man. Bob Maillard was not in the room.

"I think," said the toneless, even voice of Jachin Fell, "that all of you gentlemen had better be very careful to say only what you have seen—and know. You will kindly remain here until I have summoned the police."

He left the room, and if there were any dark implication hidden in his words, no one seemed to observe it.

Chapter 9: On The Bayou

At three o'clock in the morning a great office building is not the most desolate place on earth, perhaps; but it approaches very closely to that definition.

At three o'clock on the morning of Ash Wednesday the great white Maison Blanche building was deserted and desolate, so far as its offices were concerned. The cleaners and scrub-women had long since finished their tasks and departed. Out in the streets the tag-ends of carnival were running on a swiftly ebbing tide. A single elevator in the building was, however, in use. A single suite of offices, with carefully drawn blinds, was lighted and occupied.

They were not ornate, these offices. They consisted of two rooms, a small reception room and a large private office, both lined to the ceiling with books, chiefly law books. In the large inner room were sitting three men. One of the three, Ben Chacherre, sat in a chair tipped back against the wall, his eyes closed. From time to time he opened those sparkling black eyes of his, and through narrow-slitted lids directed keen glances at the other two men.

One of the men was the chief of police. The second was Jachin Fell, whose offices these were.

"Even if things are as you say, which I don't doubt at all," said the chief, slowly, "I can't believe the boy did it! And darn it all, if I pinch him there's goin' to be a hell of a scandal!"

Fell shrugged his shoulders, and made response in his toneless voice:

"Chief, you're up against facts. Those facts are bound to come out and the newspapers will nail your hide to the wall in a minute. You've a bare chance to save yourself by taking in young Maillard at once."

The chief chewed hard on his cigar. "I don't want to save myself by putting the wrong man behind the bars," he returned. "It sure looks like he was the Masquer all the while, but you say that he wasn't. You say this was his only job—a joke that turned out bad."

"Those are the facts," said Fell. "I don't want to accuse a man of crimes I know he did not commit. We have the best of evidence that he did commit this crime. If the newspapers fasten the entire Midnight Masquer business on him, as they're sure to do, we can't very well help it. I have no sympathy for the boy."

"Of course he did it," put in Ben Chacherre, sleepily. "Wasn't he caught with the goods?"

The others paid no heed. The chief indicated two early editions of the morning papers, which lay on the desk in front of Fell. These papers carried full accounts of the return of the Midnight Masquer's loot, explaining his robberies as part of a carnival jest.

"The later editions, comin' out now," said the chief, "will crowd all that stuff off the front page with the Maillard murder. Darn it, Fell! Whether I believe it or not, I'll have to arrest the young fool."

Chacherre chuckled. Jachin Fell smiled faintly.

"Nothing could be plainer, chief," he responded. "First, Bob Maillard comes to us in front of the opera house, and talks about a great joke that he's going to spring on his friends across the way——"

"How'd you know who he was?" interjected the chief, shrewdly.

"Gramont recognized him; Ansley and I confirmed the recognition. He was more or less intoxicated—chiefly more. Now, young Maillard was not in the room at the moment of the murder—unless he was the Masquer. Five minutes afterward he was found in a near-by room, hastily changing out of an aviator's uniform into his masquerade costume. Obviously, he had assumed the guise of the Masquer as a joke on his friends, and the joke had a tragic ending. Further, he was in the aviation service during the war, and so had the uniform ready to hand. You couldn't make anybody believe that he hasn't been the Masquer all the time!"

"Of course," and the chief nodded perplexedly. "It'd be a clear case—only you call me in and say that he *wasn't* the Masquer! Damn it, Fell, this thing has my goat!"

"What's Maillard's story?" struck in Ben Chacherre.

"He denies the whole thing," said the worried chief. "According to his story, which sounded straight the way he tells it, he meant to pull off the joke on his friends and was dressing in the Masquer's costume when he heard the shots. He claims that the shots startled him and made him change back. He swears that he had not entered the other room at all, except in his masquerade clothes. He says the murderer must have been the real Masquer. It's likely enough, because all young Maillard's crowd knew about the party that was to be held in that room during the Comus ball——"

"No matter," said Fell, coldly. "Chief, this is an open and shut case; the boy was bound to lie. That he killed his father was an accident, of course, but none the less it did take place."

"The boy's a wreck this minute." The chief held a match to his unlighted cigar. "But you say that he ain't the original Masquer?"

"No!" Fell spoke quickly. "The original Masquer was another person, and had nothing to do with the present case. This information is confidential and between ourselves."

"Oh, of course," assented the chief. "Well, I suppose I got to pull Maillard, but I hate to do it. I got a hunch that he ain't the right party."

"Virtuous man!" Fell smiled thinly. "According to all the books, the chief of police is only too glad to fasten the crime on anybody——"

"Books be damned!" snorted the chief, and leaned forward earnestly. "Look here, Fell! Do you believe in your heart that Maillard killed his father?"

Fell was silent a moment under that intent scrutiny.

"From the evidence, I am forced against my will to believe it," he said at last. "Of course, he'll be able to prove that he was not the Masquer on previous occasions; his alibis will take care of that. Up to the point of the murder, his story is all right. And, my friend, there is a chance—a very slim, tenuous chance—that his entire story is true. In that case, another person must have appeared as the Masquer which seems unlikely——"

"Or else," put in Ben Chacherre, smoothly, "the real original Masquer showed up!"

There was an instant of silence. Jachin Fell regarded his henchman with steady gray eyes. Ben Chacherre met the look with almost a trace of defiance. The chief frowned darkly.

"Yes," said the chief. "That's the size of it, Fell. You're keepin' quiet about the name of the real Masquer; why?"

"Because," said Fell, calmly, "I happen to know that he was in the auditorium at the time of the murder."

Again silence. Ben Chacherre stared at Fell, with amazement and admiration in his gaze. "When the master lies, he lies magnificently!" he murmured in French.

"Well," and the chief gestured despairingly, "I guess that lets out the real Masquer, eh?"

"Exactly," assented Fell. "No use dragging his name into it. I'll keep at work on this, chief, and if anything turns up to clear young Maillard, I'll be very glad."

"All right," grunted the chief, and rose. "I'll be on my way."

He departed. Neither Fell nor Chacherre moved or spoke for a space. When at length the clang of the elevator door resounded through the deserted corridors Ben Chacherre slipped from his chair and went to the outer door. He glanced out into the hall, closed the door, and with a nod returned to his chair.

"Well?" Jachin Fell regarded him with intent, searching eyes. "Have you any light to throw on the occasion?"

Chacherre's usual air of cool impudence was never in evidence when he talked with Mr. Fell.

"No," he said, shaking his head. "Hammond worked on the car until about nine o'clock, then beat it to bed, I guess. I quit the job at ten, and his light had been out some time. Well, master, this is a queer affair! There's no doubt that Gramont pulled it, eh?"

"You think so?" asked Fell.

Chacherre made a gesture of assent. "*Quand bois tombe, cabri monte*—when the tree falls, the kid can climb it! Any fool can see that Gramont was the man. Don't you think so yourself, master?"

Jachin Fell nodded.

"Yes. But we've no evidence—everything lies against young Maillard. Early in the morning Gramont goes to Paradis to examine that land of Miss Ledanois' along the bayou. He'll probably say nothing of this murder to Hammond, and the chauffeur may not find out about it until a day or two—they get few newspapers down there.

"Drive down to Paradis in the morning, Ben; get into touch with Hammond, and discover what time Gramont got home to-night. Write me what you find out. Then take charge of things at the Gumberts place. Make sure that every car is handled right. A headquarters man from Mobile will be here to-morrow to trace the Nonpareil Twelve that Gramont now owns."

Chacherre whistled under his breath. "What?"

Jachin Fell smiled slightly and nodded. "Yes. If Gramont remains at Paradis, I may send him on down there—I'm not sure yet. I intend to get something on that man Hammond."

"But you can't land him that way, master! He bought the car——"

"And who sold the car to the garage people? They bought it innocently." A peculiar smile twisted Fell's lips awry. "In fact, they bought it from a man named Hammond, as the evidence will show very clearly."

Ben Chacherre started, since he had sold that car himself. Then a slow grin came into his thin features—a grin that widened into a noiseless laugh.

"Master, you are magnificent!" he said, and rose. "Well, if there is nothing further on hand, I shall go to bed."

"An excellent programme," said Jachin Fell, and took his hat from the desk. "I must get some sleep myself."

They left the office and the building together.

Three hours afterward the dawn had set in—a cold, gray, and dismal dawn that rose upon a city littered with the aftermath of carnival. "Lean Wednesday" it was, in sober fact. Thus far, the city in general was ignorant of the tragedy which had taken place at the very conclusion of its gayest carnival season. Within a few hours business and social circles would be swept by the fact of Joseph Maillard's murder, but at this early point of the day the city slept. The morning papers, which to-day carried a news story that promised to shock and stun the entire community, were not yet distributed.

Rising before daylight, Henry Gramont and Hammond breakfasted early and were off by six in the car. They were well outside town and sweeping on their way to Terrebonne Parish and the town of Paradis before they realized that the day was not going to brighten appreciably. Instead, it remained very cloudy and gloomy, with a chill threat of rain in the air.

Weather mattered little to Gramont. When finally the excellent highway was left behind, and they started on the last lap of their seventy-mile ride, they found the parish roads execrable and the going slow. Thus, noon was at hand when they at length pulled into Paradis, the town closest to Lucie Ledanois' bayou land. The rain was still holding off.

"Too cold to rain," observed Gramont. "Let's hit for the hotel and get something to eat. I'll have to locate the land, which is somewhere near town."

They discovered the hotel to be an ancient structure, and boasting prices worthy of Lafitte and his buccaneers. As in many small towns of Louisiana, however, the food proved fit for a king. After a light luncheon of quail, crayfish bisque, and probably illegal venison, Gramont sighed regret that he could eat no more, and set about inquiring where the Ledanois farm lay.

There was very little, indeed, to Paradis, which lay on the bayou but well away from the railroad. It was a desolate spot, unpainted and unkept. The parish seat of Houma had robbed it of all life and growth on the one hand; on the other, the new oil and gas district had not yet touched it.

Southward lay the swamp—fully forty miles of it, merging by degrees into the Gulf. Forty miles of cypress marsh and winding bayou, uncharted, unexplored save by occasional hunters or semi-occasional sheriffs. No man knew who or what might be in those swamps, and no one cared to know. The man who brought in fish or oysters in his skiff might be a bayou fisherman, and he might be a murderer wanted in ten states. Curiosity was apt to prove extremely unhealthy. Like the Atchafalaya, where chance travellers find themselves abruptly ordered elsewhere, the Terrebonne swamps have their own secrets and know how to keep them.

Gramont had no difficulty in locating the Ledanois land, and he found that it was by no means in the swamp. A part of it, lying closer to Houma, had been sold and was now included in the new oil district; it was this portion which Joseph Maillard had sold off.

The remainder, and the largest portion, lay north of Paradis and ran along the west bank of the bayou for half a mile. A long-abandoned farm, it was high ground, with the timber well cleared off and excellently located; but tenants were hard to get and shiftless when obtained, so that the place had not been farmed for the last five years or more. After getting these facts, Gramont consulted with Hammond.

"We'd better buy some grub here in town and arrange to stay a couple of nights on the farm, if necessary," he said. "There are some buildings there, so we'll find shelter. Along the bayou are summer cottages—I believe some of them are rather pretentious places—and we ought to find the road pretty decent. It's only three or four miles out of town."

With some provisions piled in the car, they set forth. The road wound along the bayou side, past ancient 'Cajun farms and the squat homes of fishermen. Here and there had been placed camps and summer cottages, nestling amid groups of huge oaks and cypress, whose fronds of silver-gray moss hung in drooping clusters like pale and ghostly shrouds.

Watching the road closely, Gramont suddenly found the landmarks that had been described to him, and ordered Hammond to stop and turn in at a gap in the fence which had once been an entrance gate.

"Here we are! Those are the buildings off to the right. Whew! I should say it had been abandoned! Nothing much left but ruins. Go ahead!"

Before them, as they drove in from the road by a grass-covered drive, showed a house, shed, and barn amid a cluster of towering trees. Indeed, trees were everywhere about the farm, which had grown up in a regular sapling forest. The buildings were in a ruinous state—clapboards hanging loosely, roofs dotted by gaping holes, doors and windows long since gone.

Leaving the car, Gramont, followed by the chauffeur, went to the front doorway and surveyed the wreckage inside.

"What do you say, Hammond? Think we can stop here, or go back to the hotel? It's not much of a run to town——"

Hammond pointed to a wide fireplace facing them.

"I can get this shack cleaned out in about half an hour—this one room, anyhow. When we get a fire goin' in there, and board up the windows and doors, we ought to be comfortable enough. But suit yourself, cap'n! It's your funeral."

Gramont laughed. "All right. Go ahead and clean up, then, and if rain comes down we can camp here. Be sure and look for snakes and vermin. The floor seems sound, and if there's plenty of moss on the trees, we can make up comfortable beds. Too bad you're not a fisherman, or we might get a fresh fish out of the bayou——"

"I got some tackle in town," and Hammond grinned widely.

"Good work! Then make yourself at home and go to it. We've most of the afternoon before us."

Gramont left the house, and headed down toward the bayou shore.

He took a letter from his pocket, opened it, and glanced over it anew. It was an old letter, one written him nearly two years previously by Lucie Ledanois. It had been written merely in the endeavour to distract the thoughts of a wounded soldier, to bring his mind to Louisiana, away from the stricken fields of France. In the letter Lucie had described some of the more interesting features of Bayou Terrebonne—the oyster and shrimp fleets, the Chinese and Filipino villages along the Gulf, the far-spread cypress swamps; the bubbling fountains, natural curiosities, that broke up through the streams and bayous of the whole wide parish—fountains that were caused by gas seeping up from the earth's interior, and breaking through.

Gramont knew that plans were already afoot to tap this field of natural gas and pipe it to New Orleans. Oil had been found, too, and all the state was now oil-mad. Fortunes were being made daily, and other fortunes were being lost daily by those who dealt with oil-stocks instead of with oil.

"Those gas-fountains did the work!" reflected Gramont. "And according to this letter, there's one of those fountains here in the bayou, close to her property. 'Just opposite the dock,' she says. The first thing is to find the dock, then the fountain. After that, we'll decide if it's true mineral gas. If it is, then the work's done—for I'll sure take a chance on finding oil near it!"

Gramont came to the bayou and began searching his way along the thick and high fringe of bushes and saplings that girded the water's edge. Presently he came upon the ruined evidences of what had once been a small boat shed. Not far from this he found the dock referred to in the letter; nothing was left of it except a few spiles protruding from the surface of the water. But he had no need to look farther. Directly before him, he saw that which he was seeking.

A dozen feet out from shore the water was rising and falling in a continuous dome or fountain of highly charged bubbles that rose a foot above the surface. Gramont stared at it, motionless. He watched it for a space—then, abruptly, he started. It was a violent start, a start of sheer amazement and incredulity.

He leaned forward, staring no longer at the gas dome, but at the water closer inshore. For a moment he thought that his senses had deceived him, then he saw that the thing was there indeed, there beyond any doubt—a very faint trace of iridescent light that played over the surface of the water.

"It can't be possible!" he muttered, bending farther over. "Such a thing happens too rarely——"

His heart pounded violently; excitement sent the blood rushing to his brain in blinding swirls. He was gripped by the gold fever that comes upon a man when he makes the astounding discovery of untold wealth lying at his feet, passed over and disregarded by other and less-discerning men for days and years!

It was oil, no question about it. An extremely slight quantity, true; so slight a quantity that there was no film on the water, no discernible taste to the water. Gramont brought it to his mouth and rose, shaking his head.

Where did it come from? It had no connection with the gas bubbles—at least, it did not come from the dome of water and gas. How long he stood there staring Gramont did not know. His brain was afire with the possibilities. At length he stirred into action and started up the bayou bank, from time to time halting to search the water below him, to make sure that he could still discern the faint iridescence.

He followed it rod by rod, and found that it rapidly increased in strength. It must come from some very tiny surface seepage close at hand, that was lost in the bayou almost as rapidly as it came from the earth-depths. Only accidentally would a man see it—not unless he were searching the water close to the bank, and even then only by the grace of chance.

Suddenly Gramont saw that he had lost the sign. He halted.

No, not lost, either! Just ahead of him was a patch of reeds, and a recession of the shore. He advanced again. Inside the reeds he found the oily smear, still so faint that he could only detect it at certain angles. Glancing up, he could see a fence at a little distance, evidently the boundary fence of the Ledanois land; the bushes and trees thinned out here, and on ahead was cleared ground. He saw, through the bushes, glimpses of buildings.

Violent disappointment seized him. Was he to lose this discovery, after all? Was he to find that the seepage came from ground belonging to someone else? No—he stepped back hastily, barely in time to avoid stumbling into a tiny trickle of water, a rivulet that ran down into the bayou, a tributary so insignificant that it was invisible ten feet distant! And on the surface a faint iridescence.

Excitement rising anew within him, Gramont turned and followed this rivulet, his eyes aflame with eagerness. It led him for twenty feet, and ceased abruptly, in a bubbling spring that welled from a patch of low, tree-enclosed land. Gramont felt his feet sinking in grass, and saw that there was a dip in the ground hereabouts, a swampy little section all to itself. He picked a dry spot and lay down on his face, searching the water with his eyes.

Moment after moment he lay there, watching. Presently he found the slight trickle of oil again—a trickle so faint and slim that even here, on the surface of the tiny rivulet, it could be discerned only with great difficulty. A very thin seepage, concluded Gramont; a thin oil, of course. So faint a little thing, to mean so much!

It came from the Ledanois land, no doubt of it. What did that matter, though? His eyes widened with flaming thoughts as he gazed down at the slender thread of water. No matter at all where this came from—the main point was proven by it! There was oil here for the finding, oil down in the thousands of feet below, oil so thick and abundant that it forced itself up through the earth fissures to find an outlet!

"Instead of going down five or six thousand feet," he thought, exultantly, "we may have to go down only as many hundred. But first we must get an option or a lease on all the land roundabout—all we can secure! There will be a tremendous boom the minute this news breaks. If we get those options, we can sell them over again at a million per cent. profit, and even if we don't strike oil in paying quantities, we'll regain the cost of our drilling! And to think of the years this has been here, waiting for someone——"

Suddenly he started violently. An abrupt crashing of feet among the bushes, an outbreak of voices, had sounded not far away—just the other side of the boundary fence. He was wakened from his dreams, and started to rise. Then he relaxed his muscles and lay quiet, astonishment seizing him; for he heard his own name mentioned in a voice that was strange to him.

CHAPTER 10: MURDER

The voice was strange to Gramont, yet he had a vague recollection of having at some time heard it before. It was a jaunty and impudent voice, very self-assured—yet it bore a startled and uneasy note, as though the speaker had just come unaware upon the man whom he addressed.

"Howdy, sheriff!" it said. "Didn't see you in there— what you doin' so far away from Houma, eh?"

"Why, I've been looking over the place around here," responded another voice, which was dry and grim. "I know you, Ben Chacherre, and I think I'll take you along with me. Just come from New Orleans, did you?"

"Me? Take *me*?" The voice of Chacherre shrilled up suddenly in alarm. "Look here, sheriff, it wasn't me done it! It was Gramont——"

There came silence. Not a sound broke the stillness of the late afternoon.

Gramont, listening, lay bewildered and breathless. Ben Chacherre, the sneak thief—how had Chacherre come here? Gramont knew nothing of any tie between Jachin Fell and Chacherre; he could only lie in the grass and wonder at the man's presence. What "place" was it that the sheriff of Houma had been looking over? And what was it that he, Gramont, was supposed to have done?

Confused and wondering, Gramont waited. And, as he waited, he caught a soft sound from the marshy ground beside him—a faint "plop" as though some object had fallen close by on the wet grass. At the moment he paid no heed to this sound, for again the uncanny silence had fallen.

Listening, Gramont fancied that he caught slow, stealthy footsteps amid the undergrowth, but derided the fancy as sheer imagination. His brain was busy with this new problem. Houma, he knew, was the seat of the parish or county. This Ben Chacherre appeared to have suddenly and unexpectedly encountered the sheriff, to his obvious alarm, and the sheriff had for some reason decided to arrest him; so much was clear.

Chacherre had something to do with the "place"—did that mean the adjacent property, or the Ledanois farm? In his puzzled bewilderment over this imbroglio Gramont for the moment quite forgot the trickle of oil at his feet.

But now the deep silence became unnatural and sinister. What had happened? Surely, Ben Chacherre had not been arrested and taken away in such silence! Why had the voices so abruptly ceased? Vaguely uneasy, startled by the prolongation of that intense stillness, Gramont rose to his feet and peered among the trees.

The two speakers seemed to have departed; he could descry nobody in sight. A step to one side gave Gramont a view of the land adjoining the Ledanois place. This was cleared of all brush, and under some immense oaks to the far left he had a glimpse of a large summer cottage, boarded up and apparently deserted. Nearer at hand, however, he saw other buildings, and these drew his attention. He heard the throbbing pound of a motor at work, and as there was no power line along here, the place evidently had its own electrical plant. He scrutinized the scene before him appraisingly.

There were two large buildings here. One seemed to be a large barn, closed, the other was a long, low shed which was too large to be a garage. The door of this was open, and before the opening Gramont saw three men standing in talk; he recognized none of them. Two of the talkers were clad in greasy overalls, and the third figure showed the flash of a collar. The sheriff, Ben Chacherre, and some other man, thought Gramont. He would not have known Chacherre had he encountered him face to face. To him, the man was a name only.

The mention of his own name by Chacherre impelled him to go forward and demand some explanation. Then it occurred to him that perhaps he had made a mistake; it would have been very easy, for he was not certain that Chacherre had referred to him. There could be other Gramonts, or other men whose name would have much the same sound in a Creole mouth.

"I'd better attend to my own business," thought Gramont, and turned away. He noticed that the motor had ceased its work. "Wonder what rich chap can be down here at his summer cottage this time of year? May be only a caretaker, though. I'd better give all my attention to this oil, and let other things alone."

He retraced his steps to the bayou bank and turned back toward the house. As he did so, Hammond appeared coming toward him, knife in hand.

"I'm going to cut me a pole and land a couple o' fish for supper," announced the chauffeur, grinning. "Got things cleaned up fine, cap'n! You won't know the old shack."

"Good enough," said Gramont. "Here, step over this way! I want to show you something."

He led Hammond to the rivulet and pointed out the thin film of oil on the surface.

"There's our golden fortune, sergeant! Oil actually coming out of the ground! It doesn't happen very often, but it does happen—and this is one of the times. I'll not bother to look around any farther."

"Glory be!" said Hammond, staring at the rivulet. "Want to hit back for town?"

"No; we couldn't get back until sometime to-night, and the roads aren't very good for night work. I'm going to get some leases around here—perhaps I can do it right away, and we'll start back in the morning. Go ahead and get your fish."

Regaining the house, he saw that Hammond had indeed cleaned up in great style, and had the main room looking clean as a pin, with a fire popping on the hearth. He did not pause here, but went to the car, got in, and started it. He drove back to the road, and followed this toward town for a few rods, turning in at a large and very decent-looking farmhouse that he had observed while passing it on the way out.

He found the owner, an intelligent-appearing Creole, driving in some cows for milking, and was a little startled to realize that the afternoon was so late. When he addressed the farmer in French, he received a cordial reply, and discovered that this man owned the land across the road from the Ledanois place—that his farm, in fact, covered several hundred acres.

"Who owns the land next to the Ledanois place?" inquired Gramont.

"I sold that off my land a couple of years ago," replied the other. "A man from New Orleans wanted it for a summer place—a business man there, Isidore Gumberts."

Gumberts—"Memphis Izzy" Gumberts! The name flashed to Gramont's mind, and brought the recollection of a conversation with Hammond. Why, Gumberts was the famous crook of whom Hammond had spoken.

"I saw the sheriff awhile ago, heading up the road," observed the Creole. "Did you meet him?"

Gramont shook his head. "No, but I saw several men at the Gumberts place. Perhaps he was there——"

"Not there, I guess," and the farmer laughed. "Those fellows have rented the place from Gumberts, I hear; they're inventors, and quiet enough men. You're a stranger here?"

Gramont introduced himself as a friend of Miss Ledanois, and stated frankly that he was looking for oil and hoped to drill on her land.

"I'd like a lease option from you," he went on. "I don't want to buy your land at all; what I want is a right to drill for oil on it, in case any shows up on Miss Ledanois' land. It's all a gamble, you know. I'll give you a hundred dollars for the lease, and the usual eighth interest in any oil that's found. I've no lease blanks with me, but if you'll give me the option, a signed memorandum will be entirely sufficient."

The farmer regarded oil as a joke, and said so. The hundred dollars, however, and the prospective eighth interest, were sufficient to induce him to part with the option without any delay. He was only too glad to get the thing done with at once, and to pocket Gramont's money.

Gramont drove away, and was just coming to the Ledanois drive when he suddenly threw on the brakes and halted the car, listening. From somewhere ahead of him—the Gumberts place, he thought instantly—echoed a shot, and several faint shouts. Then silence again.

Gramont paused, indecisive. The sheriff was making an arrest, he thought. A hundred possibilities flitted through his brain, suggested by the sinister combination of Memphis Izzy, known even to Hammond as a prince among crooks, with this secluded place leased by "inventors." Bootlegging? Counterfeiting?

As he paused, thus, he suddenly started; he was certain that he had caught the tones of Hammond, as though in a sudden uplifted oath of anger. Gramont threw in his clutch and sent the car jumping forward—he remembered that he had left Hammond beside the rivulet, close to the Gumberts property. What had happened?

He came, after a moment of impatience, to an open gate whose drive led to the Gumberts place. Before him, as he turned in, unfolded a startling scene. Three men, the same three whom he had seen from the bushes, were standing in front of the low shed; two of them held rifles, the third, one of the "inventors" in overalls, was winding a bandage about a bleeding hand. The two rifles were loosely levelled at Hammond, who stood in the centre of the group with his arms in the air.

Whatever had happened, Hammond had evidently not been easily captured. His countenance was somewhat battered, and the one captor who wore a collar was bleeding copiously from a cut cheek. The three turned as Gramont's car drove up, and Hammond gave an ejaculation of relief.

"Here he is now——"

"Shut up!" snapped one of his armed captors in an ugly tone. "Hurry up, Chacherre—get a rope and tie this gink!"

Gramont leaped from the car and strode forward.

"What's been going on here?" he demanded, sharply. "Hammond——"

"I found a dead man over in them bushes," shot out Hammond, "and these guys jumped me before I seen 'em. They claim I done it——"

"A dead man!" repeated Gramont, and looked at the three. "What do you mean?"

"Give him the spiel, Chacherre," growled one of them. Ben Chacherre stepped forward, his bold eyes fastened on those of Gramont with a look of defiance.

"The sheriff was here some time ago, looking for a stolen boat," he said, "and went off toward the Ledanois place. We were following, in order to help him search, when we came upon this man standing in the bushes, over the body of the sheriff. A knife was in his hand, and the sheriff had been stabbed to death. He drew a pistol and shot one of us——"

Gramont was staggered for a moment. "Wait!" he exclaimed. "Hammond, how much of this is true?"

"What I'm tellin' you, cap'n," answered Hammond, doggedly. "I found a man layin' there and was looking at him when these guys jumped me. I shot that fellow in the arm, all right, then they grabbed my gun and got me down. That's all."

The sheriff—murdered!

Into the mind of Gramont leaped that brief conversation which he had overheard between Ben Chacherre and the sheriff; the strange, unnatural silence which had concluded that broken-off conversation. He stared from Hammond to the others, speechless for the moment, yet with hot words rising impetuously in him.

Now he noticed that Chacherre and his two companions were watching him very intently, and were slightly circling out. He sensed an acquaintance among all these men. He saw that the wounded man had finished his bandaging, and was now holding his unwounded hand in his jacket pocket, bulkily, menacingly.

Danger flashed upon Gramont—flashed upon him vividly and with startling clearness. He realized that anything was possible in this isolated spot—this spot where murder had so lately been consummated! He checked on his very lips what he had been about to blurt forth; at this instant, Hammond voiced the thought in his mind.

"It's a frame-up!" said the chauffeur, angrily.

"That's likely, isn't it?" Chacherre flung the words in a sneer, but with a covert glance at Gramont. "This fellow is your chauffeur, ain't he? Well, we got to take him in to Houma, that's all."

"Where's the sheriff's body?" demanded Gramont, quietly.

"Over there," Chacherre gestured. "We ain't had a chance to bring him back yet—this fellow kept us busy. Maybe you want to frame up an alibi for him?"

Gramont paid no attention to the sneering tone of this last. He regarded Chacherre fixedly, thinking hard, keeping himself well in hand.

"You say the sheriff was here, then went over toward the Ledanois land?" he asked. "Did he go alone, or were you with him?"

"We were fixin' to follow him," asserted Chacherre, confidently. This was all Gramont wanted to know—that the man was lying. "We were trailin' along after him when he stepped into the bushes. This man of yours was standing over him with a knife——"

"I was, too, when they found me—I was cuttin' me a fishpole," said Hammond, sulkily. He was plainly beginning to be impressed and alarmed by the evidence against him. Gramont only nodded.

"No one saw the actual murder, then?"

"No need for it," said Chacherre, brazenly. "When we found him that way! Eh?"

"I suppose not," answered Gramont, his eyes fastened thoughtfully on Hammond. The latter caught the look, let his jaw fall in astonishment, then flushed and compressed his lips—and waited. Gramont glanced at Chacherre, and launched a chance shaft.

"You're Ben Chacherre, aren't you? Do you work for Mr. Fell?"

The chance shot scored. "Yes," said Chacherre, his eyes narrowing.

"What are you doing here, then?"

For an instant Chacherre was off guard. He did not know how much—or little—Gramont knew; but he did know that Gramont was aware who had taken the loot of the Midnight Masquer from the luggage compartment of the car. This knowledge, very naturally, threw him back on the defence of which he was most sure.

"I came on an errand for my master," he said, and with those words gave the game into Gramont's hands.

There was a moment of silence. Gramont stood apparently in musing thought, conscious that every eye was fastened upon him, and that one false move would now spell disaster. He gave no sign of the tremendous shock that Chacherre's words had just given him; when he spoke, it was quietly and coolly:

"Then your master is evidently associated with Memphis Izzy Gumberts, who owns this place here. Is that right?"

Both Hammond and Chacherre's two friends started at this.

"I don't know anything about that," returned Chacherre, with a shrug which did not entirely conceal his uneasiness. "I know that we've got a murderer here, and that we'll have to dispose of him. Do you object?"

"Of course not," said Gramont, calmly. "Step aside and give me a moment in private with Hammond. Then by all means take him in to Houma. I'd suggest that you tie him up, or make use of handcuffs if the sheriff brought any along. Then you'd better take in the body of the sheriff also. Hammond, a word with you!"

This totally unexpected acquiescence on the part of Gramont seemed to stun Chacherre into inaction. He half moved, as though uncertain whether to bar Gramont from the prisoner, then he stepped aside as Gramont advanced. A gesture to his two companions prevented them from interfering.

"Keep 'em covered, though," he said, shifting his own rifle slightly and watching with a scowl of suspicion.

Gramont ignored him and went up to Hammond, with a look of warning.

"You'll have to submit to this, old man," he said, in a tone that the others could not overhear. "Don't dream that I'm deserting you; but I want a good look at this place if all three of them go away. They must not suspect——"

"Cap'n, look out!" broke in Hammond, urgently. "This here is a gang—the whole thing is a frame-up on me!"

"I know it—I was present when the sheriff was murdered; but keep quiet. I'll come to Houma later to-night and see you." He turned away with a shrug as though Hammond had denied him some favour, and lifted his voice. "Chacherre! How are you to take this man into town? How did you get here? Will you need to use my car?"

"No." The Creole jerked his head toward the barn. "I came in Mr. Fell's car—it's got a sprung axle and is laid up. We'll take him back in another one."

"Very well," Gramont paused and glanced around. "This is a terrible blow, men. I never dreamed that

Hammond was a murderer or could be one! You don't know of any motive for the crime?"

They shook their heads, but suspicion was dying from their eyes. Gramont glanced again at his chauffeur.

"I'll not abandon you, Hammond," he said, severely, coldly. "I'll stop in at Houma and see that you have a lawyer. I think, gentlemen, we had better attend to bringing in the body of the sheriff, eh?"

The wounded man dodged into the barn and returned with a strip of rope. Chacherre took this, and firmly bound Hammond's arms, then forced him to sit down and bound his ankles.

"You watch him," he ordered the wounded member of the trio. "We'll get the sheriff."

Allowing Chacherre and his companion to take the lead, Gramont went with them to the place where the murdered officer lay. As he went, the conviction grew more sure within him that, when he lay there by the rivulet, he had actually heard the last words uttered by the sheriff; that Chacherre had committed the murder in that moment—a noiseless, deadly stab! That Hammond could or would have done it he knew was absurd.

They found the murdered man lying among the bushes. He had been stabbed under the fifth rib—the knife had gone direct to the heart. Chacherre announced that he had Hammond's knife as evidence and Gramont merely nodded his head.

Lifting the body between them, they bore it back to the barn.

"Now," said Gramont, quickly, "I'm off for Houma—if I don't miss my road! You men will be right along?"

"In a jiffy," said Chacherre, promptly.

Gramont climbed into his car and drove away. He had no fear of anything happening to Hammond; the evidence against the latter was damning, and with three men to swear him into a hangman's noose, they would bring him to jail safe enough.

"A clever devil, that Chacherre!" he thought, grimly. "We're up against a gang, beyond any doubt. Now, if they don't suspect me——"

He turned in at the Ledanois gate, knowing himself to be beyond sight or hearing of the Gumberts place. He drove the car away from the house, and into the thick of the densest bush-growth that he could find where it was well concealed from sight. Then, on foot, he made his way along the bank of the bayou until he had come to the rivulet where oil showed.

Here he paused, concealing himself and gaining a place where he could get a view of the Gumberts land. He saw Chacherre and Hammond there, beside the body of the sheriff; the other two men were swinging open the barn door. They disappeared inside, and a moment later Gramont heard the whirr of an engine starting. A car backed out into the yard—a seven-passenger Cadillac— and halted.

The three men lifted the body of the sheriff, into the tonneau. Chacherre took the wheel, Hammond being bundled in beside him. The other two men climbed in beside the body, rifles in hand. Chacherre started the car toward the road.

"All fine!" thought Gramont with a thrill of exultation. "They've all cleared out and left the place to me—and I want a look at that place."

Suddenly, as he stood there, he remembered the slight "plump" that he had heard during that interminable silence which had followed the conversation between the sheriff and Ben Chacherre. It was a sound as though something had fallen near him in the soggy ground.

The remembrance startled him strangely. He visualized an excited murderer standing beside his victim, knife in hand; he visualized the abhorrence which must have seized the man for a moment—the abhorrence which must have caused him to do something in that moment which in a cooler time he would not have done.

Gramont turned toward the little marshy spot where he had lain listening. He bent down, searching the wet ground, heedless that the water soaked into his boots. And, after a minute, a low exclamation of satisfaction broke from him as he found what he sought.

Chapter 11: The Gangsters

Gramont left the covert and walked forward.

He was thinking about that odd mention of Jachin Fell—had Chacherre lied in saying he had come here on his master's business? Perhaps. The man had come in Fell's car, and would not hesitate to lie about using the car. For the moment, Gramont put away the circumstance, but did not forget it.

He walked openly toward the Gumberts buildings, thinking that he would have time for a good look around the place before dusk fell; he would then get off for Houma, and attend to Hammond's defence.

As for the place before him, he was convinced that it was abandoned. Had any one, other than Chacherre and his two friends, been about the buildings, the late excitement would have brought out the fact. No one had appeared, and the buildings seemed vacant.

Gramont's intent was simple and straightforward. In case he found, as he expected to find, any evidence of illegal occupation about the place—as the sheriff seemed to have discovered to his cost—he would lay Chacherre and the other two men by the heels that night in Houma. He would then go on to New Orleans and have Gumberts arrested, although he had no expectation that the master crook could be held on the murder-accessory charge. If this place were used for the lotteries, even, he was fairly certain that Memphis Izzy would have his own tracks covered. The men higher up always did.

He walked straight in upon the barn. It loomed before him, closed, lurid in the level rays of the westering sun. The doors in front had been only loosely swung together and Gramont found them unlocked. He stood in the opening, and surprise gripped him. He was held motionless, gazing with astonished wonder at the sight confronting him.

Directly before him was a small roadster, one which he remembered to have seen Jachin Fell using; in this car, doubtless, Ben Chacherre had driven from the city. He recalled the fact later, with poignant regret for a lost opportunity. But, at the present moment, he was lost in amazement at the great number of other cars presenting themselves to his view.

They were lined up as deep as the barn would hold them, crammed into every available foot of space; well over a dozen cars, he reckoned swiftly. What was more, all were cars of the highest class, with the exception of Fell's roadster. Directly before him were two which he was well aware must have cost close upon ten thousand each. What did this mean? Certainly no one man or one group of men, in this back-country spot, could expect to use such an accumulation of expensive cars!

Gramont glanced around, but found no trace of machinery in the barn. Remembering the motor that he had heard, he turned from the doorway in frowning perplexity. He strode on toward the long shed which stood closer to the house. At the end of this shed was a door, and when he tried it, Gramont found it unlocked. It swung open to his hand, and he stepped inside.

At first he paused, confused by the vague objects around, for it was quite dark in here. A moment, and his eyes grew accustomed to the gloomier lighting. Details came to him: all around were cars and fragments of cars, chassis and bodies in all stages of dismemberment. Still more cars!

He slowly advanced to a long bench that ran the length of the shop beneath the windows. A shop, indeed— a shop, he quickly perceived, fitted with every tool and machine necessary to the most complete automobile repair establishment! Even an air-brush outfit, at one end, together with a drying compartment, spoke of repaint jobs.

Comprehension was slowly dawning upon the mind of Gramont; a moment later it became certainty, when he came to a stop before an automobile engine lying on the bench. He found it to be the engine from a Stutz—the latest multi-valve type adopted by that make of car, and this particular bit of machinery looked like new.

Gramont inspected it, and he saw that the men had done their work well. The original engine number had been carefully dug out, and the place as carefully filled and levelled with metal. Beside it a new number had been stamped. A glance at the electrical equipment around showed that these workers had every appliance with which to turn out the most finished of jobs.

As he straightened up from the engine Gramont's eyes fell upon a typed sheet of paper affixed to the wall above the bench. His gaze widened as he inspected it by the failing light. Upon that paper was a list of cars. After each car was a series of numbers plainly comprising the original numbers of the engine, body, radiator, and other component parts, followed by another series of new numbers to be inserted. That sheet of paper showed brains, organizing ability, care, and attention to the last detail!

Here was the most carefully planned and thorough system of automobile thievery that Gramont had ever heard of. He stood motionless, knowing that this typed sheet of paper in itself was damning evidence against the whole gang of workers. What was more to the point, that paper could be traced; the typewriting could be traced to the man higher up—doubtless Memphis Izzy himself! These men ran in cars by the wholesale, probably from states adjacent to Louisiana. Here, at this secluded point on the bayou, they changed the cars completely about, in number, paint, style of body, and then probably got rid of the new product in New Orleans.

Gramont stood motionless. Surprise had taken hold of him, and even a feeling of slight dismay. This was not at all what he had hoped to find there. He had thought to come upon some traces of the lottery game——

"Seen all you want, bo?" said a voice behind him.

Gramont turned. He found himself gazing directly into an automatic pistol over which glittered a pair of blazing eyes. The man was a stranger to him. The place had not been deserted, after all. He was caught.

"Who are you?" demanded Gramont, quietly.

"Me?" The stranger was unsmiling, deadly. In those glittering eyes Gramont read the ferocity of an animal at bay. "I s'pose you would like to know that, huh? I guess you know enough right now to get all that's comin' to you, bo! Got any particular business here? Speak up quick!"

Gramont was silent. The other sneered at him, viciously.

"Hurry up! Turn over the name and address, and I'll notify the survivin' relatives. Name, please?"

"Henry Gramont," was the calm response. "Don't get hasty, my friend. Didn't you see me here a little while ago with Chacherre and the other boys?"

"What's that?" The glittering eyes flamed up with suspicion and distrust. "Here—with them? No, I didn't. I been away fishing all afternoon. What the hell you doing around this joint?"

"Your best scheme," said Gramont, coldly, "is to change your style of tone, and to do it in a hurry! If you don't know what's happened here this afternoon, don't ask me; you'll find out soon enough when the other boys get back. You'd better tell them I'm going to get in touch with Memphis Izzy the minute I get back to the city, and that the less talking they do——"

"What the hell's all this?" demanded the other again, but with a softening of accent. The moniker of Gumberts had its effect, and seemed to shake the man instantly. Gramont smiled as he perceived that the game was won.

"I never heard of no Gramont," went on the other, quickly. "What you doin' here?"

"You're due to learn a good many things, I imagine," said Gramont, carelessly. "As for me, I happened on the place largely by accident. I happen to be in partnership with a man named Jachin Fell, and I came out here on business——"

To Gramont's astonishment the pistol was lowered instantly. It was well that he ceased speaking, for what he had just said proved to be open to misconstruction, and if he had said any more he would have spoiled it. For the man facing him was staring at him in mingled disgust and surprise.

"You're in partnership with *the boss*!" came the astounding words. "Well, why in hell didn't you say all that in the first place, instead o' beefin' around? That's no way to butt in, and me thinking you was some dick on the job! Got anything to prove that you ain't pullin' something cute on me?"

"Do you know Fell's writing?" asked Gramont, with difficulty forcing himself to meet the situation coherently. Jachin Fell—the boss!

"I know his mitt, all right."

From his pocket Gramont produced a paper—the memorandum or agreement which he had drawn up with Fell on the previous afternoon, relating to the oil company. The other man took it and switched on an electric light bulb overhead. In this glare he was revealed as a ratty little individual with open mouth and teeth hanging out—an adenoidal type, and certainly a criminal type.

It crossed the mind of Gramont that one blow would do the work—but he stood motionless. No sudden game would help him here. The discovery that Fell was "the boss" paralyzed him completely. He had never dreamed of such a contingency. Fell, of all men!

Jachin Fell the "boss" of this establishment! Jachin Fell the man higher up—the brains behind this criminal organization! It was a perfect thunderbolt to Gramont. Now he understood why Chacherre was in the employ of

Fell—why no arrest of the man had been possible! Now he perceived that Chacherre must have told the truth about coming here on business for Fell. Reaching farther back, he saw that Fell must have received the loot of the Midnight Masquer, must have turned it over to Lucie Ledanois——

Did *she* know?

"All right, Mr. Gramont." The ratty little man turned to him with evident change of front. "We ain't takin' no chances here, y'understand. Got quite a shipment of cars comin' in from Texas, and we're tryin' to get some o' these boats cleaned out to make room. Bring out any orders?"

Gramont's brain worked fast.

By overcoming this guttersnipe he might have the whole place at his mercy—but that was not what he wanted. He suddenly realized that he had other and more important fish to fry in New Orleans. Gumberts was there. Fell was there. What he must do demanded time, and his best play was to gain all the time possible, and to prevent this gang from suspecting him in any way.

"Did you see Ben Chacherre?" he countered.

"Uh-huh—seen him just after he come. Gumberts will be out day after to-morrow, he said. The boss is framin' some sort of deal on a guy that he wants laid away—some guy name o' Hammond. Chacherre is running it. He figgers on gettin' Hammond on account of some car that's bein' hunted up——"

Gramont laughed suddenly, for there was a grim humour about the thing. So Jachin Fell wanted to "get something" on poor Hammond! And Chacherre had seized the golden opportunity that presented itself this afternoon—instead of "getting" Hammond for the theft of a car, Chacherre had coolly fastened murder upon him!

"Ben is one smart man; I expect he thinks the gods are working for him," said Gramont, thinly. "So you don't know what happened to-day, eh? Well, it's great news, but I've got no time to talk about it. They'll tell you when they get back——"

"Where'd they go?" demanded the other.

"Houma. Now listen close! Chacherre did not know that I was in partnership with the boss, get me? I didn't want to tell all the crowd in front of him. Between you and me, the boss isn't any too sure about Ben——"

"Say, I get you there!" broke in the other, sagely. "I tells him six months ago to watch out for that Creole guy!"

"Exactly. You can tell the boys about me when they come back—I don't suppose Ben will be with them. Now, I've been looking over that place next door——"

"Oh!" exclaimed the other, suddenly. "Sure! The boss said that one of his friends would be down to——"

"I'm the one—or one of them," and Gramont chuckled as he reflected on the ludicrous aspects of the whole affair. "I'm going to Houma now, and then back to the city. My car's over next door. Mr. Fell wanted me to warn you to lay low on the lottery business. He's got a notion that someone's been talking."

"You go tell the boss," retorted the other in an aggrieved tone, "to keep his eye on the guys that *can* talk! Who'd we talk to here? Besides, we're workin' our heads off on these here boats. Memphis Izzy is attending to the lottery—he's got the whole layout up to the house, and we ain't touching it, see? Tell the boss all that."

"Tell him yourself," Gramont laughed, good-humouredly. "Gumberts is coming out day after to-morrow, is he? That'll be Friday. Hm! I think that I'd better bring Fell out here the same day, if I can make it. I probably won't see Gumberts until then—I'm not working in with him and he doesn't know me yet—but I'll try and get out here on Friday with Fell. Now, I'll have to beat it in a hurry. Any message to send?"

"Not me," was the answer.

Gramont scarcely knew how he departed, until he found himself scrambling back through the underbrush of the Ledanois place.

He rushed into the house, found the fire had died down beyond all danger, and swiftly removed the few things they had taken from the car. Carrying these, he stumbled back to where he had hidden the automobile. He scarcely dared to think, scarcely dared to congratulate himself on the luck that had befallen him, until he found himself in his own car once more, and with open throttle sweeping out through the twilight toward Paradis and Houma beyond. A whirlwind of mad exultation was seething within him—exultation as sudden and tremendous as the past weeks had been uneventful and dragging!

Gramont, in common with many others, had heard much indefinite rumour of an underground lottery game that was being worked among the negroes of the state and the Chinese villages along the Gulf coast. And now he knew definitely.

Lotteries have never died out in Louisiana since the brave old days of the government-ordained gambles, laws and ordinances to the contrary. No laws can make the yellow man and the black man forego the get-rich-quick heritage of their fathers. On the Pacific coast lotteries obtain and will obtain wherever there is a Chinatown. In Louisiana the days of the grand lottery have never been forgotten. The last two years of high wages had made every Negro wealthy, comparatively speaking. The lottery mongers would naturally find them a ripe harvest for the picking. And who would gravitate to this harvest field if not the great Gumberts, the uncaught Memphis Izzy, the promoter who had never been "mugged!"

Here, at one stroke, stumbling on the thing by sheer blind accident, Gramont had located the nucleus of the whole business!

Gradually his brain cooled to the realization of what work lay before him. He was through Paradis, almost without seeing the town, and switched on his lights as he took the highway to Houma. Sober reflection seized him. Not only was this crowd of crooks working a lottery, but they were also managing a stupendous thievery of automobiles, in which cars were looted by wholesale! And the man at the head of it all, the man above Memphis Izzy and his crooks, was Jachin Fell of New Orleans.

Did Lucie Ledanois dream such a thing? No. Gramont dismissed the question at once. Fell was not an unusual type of man. There were many Jachin Fells throughout the country, he reflected. Men who applied their brains to crooked work, who kept themselves above any actual share in the work, and who profited hugely by tribute money from every crook in every crime.

To the communities in which they lived such men were patterns of all that wealthy gentlemen should be. Seldom, except perhaps in gossip of the underworld, was their connection with crime ever suspected. And—this thought was sobering to Gramont—never did they come within danger of retribution at the hands of the law. Their ramifications extended too far into politics; and the governors of some southern states have unlimited powers of pardon.

"This is a big day!" reflected Gramont, dismissing the sinister suggestion of this last thought. "A big day! What it will lead to, I don't know. Not the least of it is the financial end of it—the oil seepage! That little iridescent trickle of oil on the water means that money worries are over, both for me and for Lucie. I'm sorry that I am mixed up with Fell; I've enough money of my own to drill at least one good well, and one is all we'll need to bring in oil on that place. Well, we'll see what turns up! My first job is to make sure Hammond is safe, and to relieve his mind. I'll have to leave him in jail, I suppose——"

Why did Fell want to "get something" on Hammond? To this there was no answer.

He drove into Houma to find the town abuzz with excitement, for the news of the sheriff's murder had stirred the place wildly. Proceeding straight to the court house, Gramont encountered Ben Chacherre as he was leaving the car.

"Hello, there!" he exclaimed. "Lost my road. Where's Hammond?"

Chacherre jerked his head toward the court house.

"In yonder. Say, are you going back to the city to-night?"

"Yes." Gramont regarded him. "Why?"

"Take me back, will you? I've missed the last up train, and if you're goin' back anyhow I won't have to hire a car. I can drive for you, and we'll make it in a couple of hours, before midnight sure."

"Hop in," said Gramont, nodding toward the car. "I'll be back as soon as I've had a word with Hammond. No danger of his getting lynched, I hope?"

"Not a chance," said the other, conclusively. "Six deputies up there now, and quite a bunch of ex-soldiers comin' to stand guard. You goin' to fight the case?"

"No," said Gramont. "Can't fight a sure thing, can you? I'm sorry for him, though."

Chacherre shrugged his shoulders and got into the car.

Gramont was much relieved to find that there was no danger of lynching, which had been his one fear. It was only with much persuasion that he got past the guard and into the court house, where he was received by a number of deputies in charge of the situation.

After conferring with them at some length, he was grudgingly taken to the cell occupied by Hammond. The latter received him with a wide grin, and gave no signs of the gruelling ordeal through which he had passed.

"Listen, old man," said Gramont, earnestly. "Will you play out the game hard to the end? I'll have to leave you here for two days. At the end of that time you'll be free."

The listening deputies sniffed, but Hammond merely grinned again and put a hand through the bars.

"Whatever you say, cap'n," he rejoined. "It sure looks bad——"

"Don't you think it," said Gramont, cheerfully. "A lot of things have happened since I saw you last! I've got the real murderer right where I want him—but I can't have him arrested yet."

"It's a gang," said Hammond. "You watch out, cap'n, I heard 'em say somethin' about Memphis Izzy—remember the guy I told you about one day? Well, this is no piker's game! We're up against somethin' solid——"

"I know it," and Gramont nodded. He turned to the deputies. "Gentlemen, you have my address if you wish to communicate with me. I shall be back here day after to-morrow—at least, before midnight of that day. I warn you, that if anything happens to this man in the meantime, you shall be held personally responsible. He is innocent."

"Looks like we'd better hold you, too," said one of the men. "You seem to know a lot!"

Gramont looked at him a moment.

"I know enough to tell you where to head in if you try any funny work here," he said, evenly. "Gentlemen, thank you for permitting the interview! I'll see you later."

The coroner's jury had already adjudged Hammond guilty of the murder. Returning to the car, Gramont had Ben Chacherre drive to a restaurant, where they got a bite to eat. Twenty minutes later they were on their way to New Orleans—and Gramont learned for the first time of Joseph Maillard's murder by the Midnight Masquer, and of the arrest of Bob Maillard for the crime.

CHAPTER 12: THE ULTIMATUM

Upon the following morning Gramont called both Jachin Fell and Lucie Ledanois over the telephone. He acquainted them briefly with the result of his oil investigation, and arranged a meeting for ten o'clock, at Fell's office.

It was slightly before ten when Gramont called with the car for Lucie. Under the spell of her smiling eagerness, the harshness vanished from his face; it returned again a moment later, for he saw that she, too, was changed. There was above them both a cloud. That of Gramont was secret and brooding. As for Lucie, she was in mourning. The murder of Joseph Maillard, the arrest and undoubted guilt of Bob Maillard, dwarfed all else in her mind. Even the news of the oil seepage, and the fact that she was probably now on the road to wealth, appeared to make little impression upon her.

"Thank heaven," she said, earnestly, as they drove toward Canal Street, "that so far as you are concerned, Henry, the Midnight Masquer affair was all cleared up before this tragedy took place! It was fearfully imprudent of you——"

"Yes," answered Gramont, soberly, reading her thought. "I can realize my own folly now. If this affair were to be laid at my door, some kind of a case might be made up against me, and it would seem plausible. But, fortunately, I was out of it in time. Were we merely characters in a standardized detective story, I suppose I'd be arrested and deluged with suspense and clues and so forth."

"Your escape was too narrow to joke over, Henry," she reproved him, gravely.

"I'm not joking, my dear Lucie. I learned nothing about the tragedy until late last night. From what I can find in the papers, it seems agreed that Bob was not the real Masquer, but had assumed that guise for a joke. A tragic joke! Since he was undoubtedly drunk at the time, his story can't be relied upon as very convincing. And yet, it's frightfully hard to believe that, even by accident, a son should have shot down his own father——"

"Don't!" Lucie winced a little. "In spite of all the evidence against him, in spite of the way he was found with that aviation uniform, it's still awful to believe. I can't realize that it has actually happened."

"According to the papers, poor Mrs. Maillard has gone to pieces. No wonder."

"Yes. I was there with her all day yesterday, and shall go again to-day. They say Bob is terribly broken up. He sent for his mother, and she refused to see him. I don't know how it is all going to end! Do you think his story might be true—that somebody else might have acted as the Masquer that night?"

Gramont shook his head.

"It's possible," he said, reluctantly, "yet it hardly seems very probable. And now, Lucie, I'm very sorry indeed to say it—but you must prepare yourself against another shock in the near future."

"What do you mean? About the oil——"

"No. It's too long a story to tell you now; here we are at the Maison Blanche. Just remember my words, please. It's something that I can't go into now."

"Very well. Henry! Do you think that it's possible your chauffeur, Hammond, could have learned about the drinking party, and could have——"

Gramont started. "Hammond? No. I'll answer for him beyond any question, Lucie. By the way, does Fell know anything about Hammond having been the first Masquer?"

"Not from me," said the girl, watching him.

"Very well. Hammond got into a bit of trouble at Houma, and I had to leave him there. It was none of his fault, and he'll get out of it all right. Well, come along up to our oil meeting! Forget your troubles, and don't let my croakings about a new shock cause you any worry just yet."

He was thinking of Jachin Fell, and the girl's closeness to Fell. Had he not known that Fell was responsible for Hammond's being in jail, he might have felt differently. As it was, he was now fore-warned and fore-armed, although he could not see what animus Fell could possibly have against Hammond.

It was lucky, he reflected grimly, that he had never breathed to a soul except Lucie the fact that Hammond had been the first Masquer! Had Fell known this fact, his desire to lay Hammond by the heels might have been easily fulfilled—and Hammond would probably have found himself charged with Maillard's murder.

They found Jachin Fell dictating to a stenographer. He greeted them warmly, ushering them at once into his private office.

Gramont found it difficult to convince himself that his experiences of the previous afternoon had been real. It was almost impossible to believe that this shy, apologetic little man in gray was in reality the "man higher up!" Yet he knew it to be the case—knew it beyond any escape.

"By the way," and Fell turned to Gramont, "if you'll dictate a brief statement concerning that oil seepage, I'd be obliged! Merely give the facts. I may have need of such a statement from you."

Gramont nodded and joined the stenographer in the outer office where he dictated a brief statement. It did not occur to him that there might be danger in this; at the moment, he was rather off his guard. He was thinking so much about his future assault on Fell that he quite ignored the possibility of being placed on the defensive.

Within five minutes he had returned to Lucie and Jachin Fell, who were discussing the condition of Mrs.

Maillard. Gramont signed the statement and handed it to Fell, who laid it with other papers at his elbow.

"I suppose we may proceed to business?" began Fell. "I have drawn up articles of partnership; we can apply for incorporation later if we so desire. Lucie, both Henry Gramont and I are putting twenty-five thousand dollars into this company, while you are putting in your land, which I am valuing at an equal amount. The stock, therefore, will be divided equally among us. That is understood?"

"Yes. It's very good of you, Uncle Jachin," said the girl, quietly. "I'll leave everything to your judgment."

The little gray man smiled.

"Judgment is a poor horse to ride, as Eliza said when she crossed the ice. Here's everything in black and white. I suggest that you both glance over the articles, sign up, and we will then hold our first meeting."

Gramont and Lucie read over the partnership agreement, and found it perfectly correct.

"Very well, then, the meeting is called to order!" Jachin Fell smiled as he rapped on the desk before him. "Election of officers—no, wait! The first thing on hand is to give our company a name. Suggestions?"

"I was thinking of that last night," said Lucie, smiling a little. "Why not call it the 'American Prince Oil Company'?" And her eyes darted to Gramont merrily.

"Excellent!" exclaimed Jachin Fell. "My vote falls with yours, my dear—I'll fill in the blanks with that name. Now to the election of officers."

"I nominate Jachin Fell for president," said Gramont, quickly.

"Seconded!" exclaimed the girl, gaily, a little colour in her pale cheeks.

"Any other nominations? If not, so approved and ordered," rattled Fell, laughingly. "For the office of treasurer——"

"Miss Lucie Ledanois!" said Gramont. "Move nominations be closed."

"Seconded and carried by a two-thirds vote of stockholders," chirped Fell in his toneless voice. "So approved and ordered. For secretary——"

"Our third stockholder," put in Lucie. "He'll have to be an officer, of course!"

"Seconded and carried. So approved and ordered." Mr. Fell rapped on the table. "We will now have the report of our expert geologist in further detail than yet given."

Gramont told of finding the oil; he was not carried away by the gay mock-solemnity of Jachin Fell, and he remained grave. He went on to relate how he had secured the lease option upon the adjoining land, and suggested that other such options be secured at once upon other property in the neighbourhood. He handed the option to Fell, who laid it with the other documents.

"And now I have a proposal of my own to make," said Jachin Fell. He appeared sobered, as though influenced by Gramont's manner. "Although we've actually found oil on the place, there is no means of telling how much we'll find when we drill, or what quality it will be. Is that not correct, Mr. Gramont?"

"Entirely so," assented Gramont. "The chances are, of course, that we'll find oil in both quality and quantity. On the other hand, the seepage may be all there is. Oil is a gamble from start to finish. Personally, however, I would gamble heavily on this prospect."

"Naturally," said Mr. Fell. "However, I have been talking over the oil business with a number of men actively engaged in it in the Houma field. I think that I may safely say that I can dispose of the mineral rights to our company's land, together with this lease option secured yesterday on the adjoining land, for a sum approximating one hundred and fifty thousand dollars; reserving to our company a sixteenth interest in any oil located on the property. Personally, I believe this can be done, and I am willing to undertake the negotiations if so empowered by a note of our stockholders. Lucie, you do not mind if we smoke, I know? Let me offer you a cigar, Mr. Gramont."

Gramont took one of the El Reys offered him, and lighted it amid a startled silence. Fell's proposal came to him as a distinct shock, and already he was viewing it in the light of prompt suspicion.

"Why," exclaimed Lucie, wide-eyed, "that would be fifty thousand dollars to each of us, and not a cent expended!"

"In case it went through on that basis," added Jachin Fell, his eyes on Gramont, "I would vote that the entire sum go to Miss Ledanois. Her land alone is involved. If she then wishes to invest with us in a new company to exploit other fields, well and good. One moment, my dear! Do not protest this suggestion. The sixteenth interest reserved to our company would provide both Mr. Gramont and me with a substantial reward for our slight activity in the matter. Don't forget that interest, for it might amount to a large figure."

"Right," assented Gramont. "I would second your vote, Mr. Fell; I think the idea very just and proper that Miss Ledanois should receive the entire amount."

Lucie seemed a trifle bewildered.

"But—but, Henry!" she exclaimed. "What do you think of selling the lease to these other men?"

Gramont eyed the smoke from his cigar reflectively, quite conscious that Mr. Fell was regarding him very steadily.

"I can't answer for you, Lucie," he said at last. "I would not presume to advise."

Mr. Fell looked slightly relieved. Lucie, however, persisted.

"What would you do, then, if you were in my place?"

Gramont shrugged his shoulders.

"In that case," he said, slowly, "I would gamble. We know oil is in that ground; we know that it has been found in large quantities at Houma or near there. To my mind there is no doubt whatever that under your land lies a part of the same oil field—and a rich one. To sell fifteen-sixteenths of that oil for a hundred and fifty thousand is to give it away. I would sooner take my chances on striking a twenty-thousand barrel gusher and having the whole of it to myself. However, by all means disregard my words; this is not my affair."

Lucie glanced at Jachin Fell.

"You think it is the best thing to do; Henry does not," mused the girl. "I know that you're both thinking of me— of getting that money for me. Just the same, Uncle Jachin, I—I won't be prudent! I'll gamble! Besides," she added with smiling naivete, "I'm not a bit willing to give up having a real oil company the very minute it is formed! So we'll outvote you, Uncle Jachin."

Despite their tension, the two men smiled at her final words.

"That motion of mine has not yet been made," said Fell. Her rejection of his proposal had no effect upon his shyly smooth manner. "Will you excuse us one moment, Lucie? If I may speak with you in the outer office, Mr. Gramont, I would like to show you some confidential matters which might influence your decision in this regard."

Lucie nodded and leaned back in her chair.

Gramont accompanied Fell to the outer office, where Fell sent the stenographer to keep Lucie company. When the door had closed and they were alone, Fell took a chair and motioned Gramont to another. A cold brusquerie was evident in his manner.

"Gramont," he said, briskly, "I am going to make that motion, and I want you to vote with me against Lucie. Unfortunately, I have only a third of the voting power. I might argue Lucie into agreement, but she is a difficult person to argue with. So I mean that you shall vote with me—and I'm going to put my cards on the table before you."

"Ah!" Gramont regarded him coolly. "Your cards will have to be powerful persuaders!"

"They are," returned Jachin Fell. "I have been carefully leading up to this point—the point of selling. I have practically arranged the whole affair. I propose to sell the mineral rights in that land, largely on the strength of the signed statement you gave me a few moments ago. That statement is going to be given wide publicity, and it will be substantiated by other reports on the oil seepage."

"You interest me strangely." Gramont leaned back in his chair. The eyes of the two men met and held in cold challenge, cold hostility. "What's your motive, Fell?"

"I'll tell you: it's the interest of Lucie Ledanois." In the gaze of Fell was a strange earnestness. In those pale gray eyes was now a light of fierce sincerity which startled and warned Gramont. Fell continued with a trace of excitement in his tone.

"I've known that girl all her life, Gramont, and I love her as a father. I loved her mother before her—in a different way. I can tell you that at this moment Lucie is poor. Her house is mortgaged; she does not know, in fact, just how poor she really is. Of course, she will accept no money from me in gift. But for her to get a hundred and fifty thousand in a business deal will solve all her problems, set her on her feet for life!"

"I see," said Gramont with harsh impulse. "What do you get out of it?"

He regretted the words instantly. Fell half rose from his chair as though to answer them with a blow. Gramont, aware of his mistake, hastened to retract it.

"Forgive me, Fell," he said, quickly. "That was an unjust insinuation, and I know it. Yet, I can't find myself in agreement with you. I'm firmly set in the belief that a fortune in oil will be made off that land of Lucie's. I simply can't agree to sell out for a comparative pittance, and I'll fight to persuade her against doing it! As I look at it, the thing would not be just to her. I'm thinking, as you are, only of her interest."

A light of sardonic mockery glittered in the pale eyes of Jachin Fell.

"You are basing your firm conviction," he queried, "very largely upon your discovery of the free oil?"

"To a large extent, yes."

"I thought you would," and Fell laughed harshly.

"What do you mean?"

"I mean," said the other, fiercely earnest, "that for a month I've worked to sell that land! I had young Maillard hooked and landed—it would have been poetic justice to make him hand over a small fortune to Lucie! But that deal is off, since he's in jail. And do you know why young Maillard wanted to buy the land? For the same reason you don't want to sell. I sent him out there and he saw that oil seepage, as I meant that he should! He thought he would skin Lucie out of her land, not dreaming that I had prepared a nice little trap to swallow him. And now you come along——"

"Man, what are you driving at?" exclaimed Gramont. He was startled by what he read in the other man's face.

"Merely that I planted that oil seepage myself—or had it done by men I could trust," said Jachin Fell, calmly. He sat back in his chair and took up his cigar with an air of finality. "The confession is shameless. I love Lucie more than my own ethical purity. Besides, I intend to wrong no one in the matter."

Gramont sat stunned beyond words. The oil seepage— a plant!

The thing could have been very easily done, of course. As he sat silent there unfolded before him the motives that underlay Fell's entire action. The amazing disclosure of Jachin Fell's intrigue to enrich the girl left him bewildered. This, coupled with what he had learned on the preceding day about Jachin Fell, put his own course of action into grave perplexity.

There was no reason to doubt what Fell said. Gramont believed the little man sincere in his love for Lucie.

"No matter what the outcome, your reputation will not be affected," said Fell, quietly. "The company which will buy this land of Lucie's is controlled by me. You understand? Even if no oil is ever found there, I shall see to it that you will not be injured because of that signed statement."

Gramont nodded dull comprehension. He realized that Fell had devised this whole business scheme with infernal ingenuity; had devised it in order to take a hundred and fifty thousand dollars out of his own pocket and put it into that of Lucie. It was a present which the girl would never accept as a gift, but which, if it came in the way of business, would make her financially independent. Nobody would be defrauded. There was no chicanery about it. The thing was straight enough.

"That's not quite all of my plan," pursued Fell, as though reading Gramont's unuttered thoughts. "The minute this news becomes public, the minute your statement is published, there will be a tremendous boom in that whole section. I shall take charge of Lucie's money, and within three weeks I should double it, treble it, for her. Before the boom bursts she will be out of it all, and wealthy. Now, my dear Gramont, I do not presume that you will still refuse to vote with me? I have been quite frank, you see."

Gramont stirred in his chair.

"Yes!" he said, low-voiced. "Yes, by heavens, I do refuse!"

With an effort he checked hotly impulsive words that were on his tongue. One word now might ruin him. He dared not say that he did not want to see Fell's money pass into the hands of Lucie—money gained by fraud and theft and crime! He dared not give his reasons for refusing. He meant now to crush Fell utterly—but one wrong word would give the man full warning. He must say nothing.

"It's not straight work, Fell. Regardless of your motives, I refuse to join you."

Jachin Fell sighed slightly, and laid down his cigar with precision.

"Gramont," his voice came with the softly purring menace of a tiger's throat-tone, "I shall now adjourn this company meeting for two days, until Saturday morning, in order to give you a little time to reconsider. To-day is Thursday. By Saturday——"

"I need no time," said Gramont.

"But you will need it. I suppose you know that Bob Maillard has been arrested for parricide? You are aware of the evidence against him—all circumstantial?"

Gramont frowned. "What has that got to do with our present business?"

"Quite a bit, I fancy." A thin smile curved the lips of Jachin Fell. "Maillard is not guilty of the murder—but you are."

"Liar!" Gramont started from his chair as those three words burned into him. "Liar! Why, you know that I went home——"

"Ah, wait!" Fell lifted his hand for peace. His voice was calm. "Ansley and I both saw you depart, certainly. We have since learned that you did not reach home until some time after midnight. You have positively no alibi, Gramont. You may allege, of course, that you were wandering the streets——"

"As I was!" cried Gramont, heatedly.

"Then prove it, my dear fellow; prove it—if you can. Now, we shall keep Lucie out of all this. What remains? I know that you were the Midnight Masquer. My man, Ben Chacherre, can prove by another man who accompanied him that the Masquer's loot was taken from your car. A dictograph in the private office, yonder, has a record of the talk between us of the other morning, in which you made patent confession to being the Masquer.

"Once let me hand this array of evidence over to the district attorney, and you will most certainly stand trial. And, if you do stand trial, I can promise you faithfully that you will meet conviction. I have friends, you see, and many of them are influential in such small matters."

It was not a nice smile that curved the lips of Fell.

Gramont choked back any response, holding himself to silence with a firm will. He dared say nothing, lest he say too much. He saw that Fell could indeed make trouble for him—and that he must strike his own blow at Fell without great delay. It was a battle, now; a fight to the end.

Fell regarded Gramont cheerfully, seeming to take this crushed silence as evidence of his own triumph.

"Further," he added, "your man Hammond is now in jail at Houma, as you know, for the murder of the sheriff. Now, my influence is not confined to this city, Gramont, I may be able to clear Hammond of this charge—if you decide to vote with me. I may keep what I know about the Midnight Masquer from the press and from the district attorney—if you decide to vote with me. You comprehend?"

Gramont nodded. He saw now why Fell wanted to "get something" on Hammond. Fell had rightly reasoned that Gramont would do more to save Hammond than to save himself.

"You think I murdered Maillard, then?" he asked.

"Gramont, I don't know what to think, and that's the honest truth!" answered Fell, with a steady regard. "But I am absolutely determined to put this oil deal across, to make Lucie Ledanois at least independent, if not wealthy. I can do it, I've made all my plans to do it, and—I *will* do it!

"We'll hold another meeting day after to-morrow—Saturday morning." Fell rose. "That will give me time to conclude all arrangements. I trust, Mr. Gramont, that you will vote with me for the adjournment?"

"Yes," said Gramont, dully. "I will."

"Thank you," and Jachin Fell bowed slightly, not without a trace of mockery in his air.

CHAPTER 13: THE COIN FALLS HEADS

Gramont sat in his own room that afternoon. It seemed to him that he had been away from the city for weeks and months. Yet only a day had intervened. He sat fingering the only piece of mail that had come to him—a notice from the post of the American Legion which he had joined, to the effect that there would be a meeting that Thursday evening. Only Thursday! And to-morrow was Friday.

If he was to effect anything against the headquarters of Fell's gang he must act on the morrow or not at all. Gumberts was to be out there to-morrow. Gumberts would talk with the ratty little man of the projecting teeth and adenoids, would find Gramont had imposed upon the fellow, and there would be upheavals. The gang would take to flight, certainly, or at least make certain that Gramont's mouth was shut.

He sat fingering the postal from the Legion, and turning over events in his mind. Against Fell he had particular animosity. All that the little gray man had done had been done with the thought of Lucie Ledanois as a spur.

"Yet he can't realize that Lucie wouldn't have the money if she knew that it came from criminal sources," he thought, smiling bitterly. "He's been scheming a long time to make a fortune for her, and now he's determined to push it through regardless of me. It was clever of him to jail Hammond! He guessed that I'd do a great deal to save the redhead—more even than to save myself. Mighty clever! And now he's pretty sure that he's got me between a cleft stick, where I can't wriggle.

"If I'm to strike a blow, I'll have to do it to-morrow— before noon to-morrow, also. I'll have to leave here mighty early, and get there before Gumberts does. What was it Hammond said that day about him—that nobody in the country had ever caught Memphis Izzy? I bet I could do it, and his whole gang with him—if I knew how. There's the rub! Fell won't hesitate a minute in having me arrested. And as he said, once he got me arrested, I'd be gone. He must be able to exert powerful influence, that man!"

Should he strike or not? If he struck, he might expect the full weight of Jachin Fell's vengeance—unless his blow would include Fell among the victims.

Gramont was still pondering this dilemma when Ben Chacherre arrived.

Gramont heard the man's voice on the stairs. Ben's impudence, perhaps added to his name and the Creole French upon his lips, had carried him past the concierge unannounced, although not without a continued exchange of repartee that served to give Gramont warning of the visitor. Smiling grimly, Gramont drew a coin from his pocket, and flipped it.

The coin fell heads. He pocketed it again as Ben Chacherre knocked, and opened the door.

"Ah, Chacherre!" he exclaimed. "Come in."

Ben swaggered inside and closed the door.

"Brought a message for you, Mr. Gramont," he said, jauntily, and extended a note.

Gramont tore open the envelope and read a curt communication:

> Kindly let me know your answer as soon as possible. By to-morrow evening at the latest. It will be necessary to arrange affairs for Saturday.
> JACHIN FELL.

To arrange affairs! Fell was taking for granted that Gramont would give an assent, under force of persuasion, to the scheme. He would have everything in readiness, and if assured by Friday night of Gramont's assent, would then pull his strings and perhaps complete the whole deal before the following Monday.

The meeting of the company had been adjourned to Saturday morning. Gramont thought a moment, then went to his buhl escritoire and opened it. Chacherre had already taken a seat. Gramont wrote:

MY DEAR MR. FELL,

If you will arrange the company meeting for to-morrow evening, say nine o'clock, at your office, I think that everything may then be arranged. As I may not see Miss Ledanois in the meantime, will you be kind enough to assure her presence at the meeting?

He addressed an envelope to Fell's office, and then stamped and pocketed it.

"Well, Chacherre," he said, rising and returning to the Creole, "any further news from Houma? They haven't found the real murderer yet?"

The other came to his feet with an exclamation of surprise. As he did so, Gramont's fist caught him squarely on the point of the jaw.

Chacherre crumpled back across his chair, senseless for the moment.

"I'm afraid to take any chances with you, my fine bird," said Gramont, rubbing his knuckles. "You're too clever by far, and too handy with your weapons!"

He obtained cloths, and firmly bound the ankles and wrists of Chacherre. Not content with this, he placed the man in the chair and tied him to it with merciless knots. As he was finishing his task, Chacherre opened his eyes and gazed rapidly around.

"Awake at last, are you?" said Gramont, genially. He got his pipe, filled and lighted it. The eyes of Chacherre were now fastened upon him venomously. "Too bad for you, Chacherre, that the coin fell heads up! That spelled action."

"Are you crazy?" muttered the other in French. Gramont laughed, and responded in the same tongue.

"It does look that way, doesn't it? You're slippery, but now you're caught."

Chacherre must have realized that he stood in danger. He checked a curse, and regarded Gramont with a steady coolness.

"Be careful!" he said, his voice deadly. "What do you mean by this?"

Gramont looked at him and puffed his pipe.

"The game's up, Ben," he observed. "I know all about the place down there—about the cars, and about the lottery. Your gang has had a pleasant time, eh? But now you and the others are going to do a little work for the state on the road gangs."

"Bah! *Ca? va rive dans semaine quatte zheudis!*" spat Chacherre, contemptuously. "That will happen in the week of four Thursdays, you fool! So you know about things, eh? My master will soon shut your mouth!"

"He can't," said Gramont, placidly. "You'll all be under arrest."

Chacherre laughed scornfully, then spoke with that deadly gravity.

"Look here—you're a stranger here? Well, since you know so much, I'll tell you more! We can't be arrested, and even if you get us pinched, we'll never be convicted. Do you understand? We have influence! There are men here in New Orleans, men in the legislature, men at Washington, who will never see us molested!"

"They'll be surprised," said Gramont, although he felt that the man's words were true. "But not all of them are your friends, Ben. I don't think the governor of the state is in your gang. He's a pretty straight man, Ben."

"He's a fool like you! What is he? A puppet! He can do nothing except pardon us if the worst happens. You can't touch us."

"Well, maybe not," agreed Gramont, tapping at his pipe. "Maybe not, but we'll see! You seem mighty sure of where you stand, Ben."

Encouraged, Ben Chacherre laughed insolently.

"Let me loose," he commanded. "Or else you'll go over the road for the Midnight Masquer's work! My master has a dictograph in his office, and has your confession on record."

"So?" queried Gramont, his brows lifted. "You seem much in Mr. Fell's confidence, Ben. But I think I'll leave you tied up a little while. Memphis Izzy is going down to his summer cottage to-morrow, isn't he? I'll be there—but you won't. By the way, I think I'd better look through your pockets."

Ben Chacherre writhed suddenly, hurling a storm of curses at Gramont.

The latter, unheeding the contortions of his captive, searched the man thoroughly. Except for a roll of money, the pockets gave up little of interest. The only paper Gramont secured was a fresh telegraph blank. He would have passed this unheeded had he not noted a snaky flitting of Chacherre's eyes to it.

"Ah!" he said, pleasantly. "You appear to be interested in this, Ben. Pray, what is the secret?"

Chacherre merely glared at him in silence. Gramont inspected the blank, and a sudden exclamation broke from him. He held the bit of yellow paper to the light at varying angles.

"It's the most natural thing in the world," he said after a moment, "for a man to walk into a telegraph office, write out his telegram, and then find that he's torn two blanks instead of one from the pad on the desk. Eh? I've done it, often—and I've always put the extra blank into my pocket, Ben, thinking it might come in handy; just as you did, eh? Now let's see!

"You were excited when you wrote this, weren't you? You'd just thought of something very important, and you took care of it hurriedly—that made you jab down your pencil pretty hard. Who's Dick Hearne at Houma? An agent of the gang there?"

Chacherre merely glared, sullenly defiant. Word by word, Gramont made out the message:

Burn bundle under rear seat my car. Have done at once.

Gramont looked up and smiled thinly.

"Your car? Why, you left it in the garage at Gumberts' place, eh? That little roadster of Fell's, with the extra seat behind. If you'd been just a little bit cooler yesterday, Ben, you would have made fewer mistakes. It never occurred to you that other people might have been there in the bushes when the sheriff was murdered, eh?"

Chacherre went livid.

"It was another mistake to throw away your knife after you killed him," pursued Gramont, reflectively. "You should have held on to that knife, Ben. There's no blood, remember, on Hammond's knife—a hard thing for you and your friends to explain plausibly. Yet your knife is heavy with blood, which tests will show to be human blood. Also, the knife has your name on it; quite a handsome knife, too. On the whole, you must admit that you bungled the murder from start to finish——"

Chacherre broke in with a frightful oath—a frantically obscene storm of curses. So furious were his words that Gramont very efficiently gagged him with cloths, gagged him hard and fast.

"You also bungled when you forgot all about burning that bundle, in your excitement over getting Hammond jailed for the murder," he observed, watching Chacherre writhe. "No, you can't get loose, Ben. You'll suffer a little between now and the time of your release, but I really can't spare much pity on you.

"I think that I'll send another wire to Dick Hearne on this blank which you so thoughtfully provided. I'll order him, in your name, not to burn that bundle after all; I fancy it may prove of some value to me. And I'll also tell your friend—I suppose he has some familiar cognomen, such as Slippery Dick—to meet Henry Gramont at Houma early in the morning. I'd like to gather Dick in with the other gentlemen. I'll mention that you were kind enough to supply a few names and incidents."

At this last Ben Chacherre writhed anew, for it was a shrewd blow. He and his friends belonged to that class of crook which never "peaches." If by any mischance one of this class is jailed and convicted, he invariably takes his medicine silently, knowing that the whole gang is behind him, and that when he emerges from prison he will be sure to find money and friends and occupation awaiting him.

To know that he would be placed, in the estimation of the gang, in the same class with stool-pigeons, must have bitten deeper into Ben Chacherre than any other lash. He stared at Gramont with a frightful hatred in his blazing eyes—a hatred which gradually passed into a look of helplessness and of impotent despair.

Gramont, meantime, was writing out the telegram to Dick Hearne. This finished, he got his hat and coat, and from the bureau drawer took an automatic pistol, which he pocketed. Then he smiled pleasantly at his prisoner.

"I'll be back a little later, Ben, and I'll probably bring a friend with me—a friend who will sit up with you to-night and take care of your health. Kind of me, eh? It's getting late in the afternoon, but I don't think that it will harm you to go without any dinner. I'll 'phone Mr. Fell that you said you'd be away for a few hours, eh?

"This evening, Ben, I think that I'll attend a meeting of my post of the American Legion. You don't belong to that organization by any chance? No, I'm quite sure you don't. Very few of your exclusive acquaintances do belong. Well, see you later! Work on those bonds all you like— you're quite safe. I'm curious to see what is in that bundle under the rear seat of your car; I have an idea that it may prove interesting. Good afternoon!"

Gramont closed the door, and left the house.

Going downtown, he mailed the letter to Fell, confident that the latter would receive it on the following morning; but he did not telephone Fell. He preferred to leave the absence of Chacherre unexplained, rightly judging that Fell would not be particularly anxious about the man. It was now Thursday evening. The meeting of the oil company would be held at nine on Friday evening. Between those two times Gramont figured on many things happening.

He chuckled as he sent the telegram to Dick Hearne at Houma—a telegram signed with the name Chacherre, instructing Hearne not to burn the bundle, but to meet Gramont early in the morning at Houma. He had a very shrewd idea that this Dick Hearne might prove an important person to dispose of, and quite useful after he had been disposed of. In this conjecture he was right.

CHAPTER 14: CHACHERRE'S BUNDLE

It was seven in the morning when Henry Gramont drove his car into Houma.

In the wire which he had sent over Chacherre's signature he had commanded Dick Hearne to meet Gramont at about this time at a restaurant near the court house. Putting his car at the curb, Gramont went into the restaurant and ordered a hasty breakfast. He had brought with him copies of the morning papers, and was perusing the accounts of Bob Maillard's pitifully weak story regarding his father's murder, when a stranger stopped beside him.

"Gramont?" said the other. "Thought it was you. Hearne's my name—I had orders to meet you. What's up?"

The other man dropped into the chair opposite Gramont, who put away his papers. Hearne was a sleek individual of pasty complexion who evidently served the gang in no better light than as a go-between and runner of errands. That he suspected nothing was plain from his casual manner, although he had never seen Gramont previously.

"Business," said Gramont, leaning back to let the waitress serve his breakfast. When she had departed, he attacked it hungrily. "You got Chacherre's wire about the stuff in his car? Was it burned?"

"No. He countermanded it just as I was hirin' a car to go over to Paradis," said Hearne. "What's stirrin', anyhow?"

"Plenty. Memphis Izzy's coming down to-day. When'll he get in?"

"He'll go direct to the other place, won't come here. Oh, I reckon he'll get there along about nine this morning. Why?"

"We'll have to go over there to meet him," said Gramont. "I stopped in here to pick you up. Hammond is still safe in jail?"

"Sure." Hearne laughed evilly. "I don't guess he'll get out in a hurry, neither!"

"Chacherre was pinched last night for the murder," said Gramont, watching the other.

"The hell!" Hearne looked astonished, then relaxed and laughed again. "Some fly cop will sure lose his buttons, then! They ain't got nothin' on him."

"I heard they had plenty."

"Don't worry." Hearne waved a hand grandiloquently. "The boss is solid with the bunch up to Baton Rouge, and they'll take care of everybody. So old Ben got pinched, huh? That's one joke, man!"

Gramont's worst suspicions were confirmed by the attitude of Hearne, who plainly considered that the entire gang had nothing to fear from the law. Chacherre's boasts were backed up solidly. It was obvious to Gramont that the ramifications of the gang extended very high up indeed.

"Better cut out the talk," he said, curtly, "until we get out of here."

Hearne nodded and rolled a cigarette.

When his hasty meal was finished Gramont paid at the counter and led the way outside. He motioned toward the car, and Hearne obediently climbed in, being evidently of so little account in the gang that he was accustomed to taking orders from everyone.

Gramont headed out of town and took the Paradis road. Before he had driven a mile, however, he halted the car, climbed out, and lifted one side of the hood.

"Give me those rags from the bottom of the car, Hearne," he said, briefly.

The other obeyed. As Gramont made no move to come and get them, Hearne got out of the car; then Gramont rose from the engine unexpectedly, and Hearne looked into a pistol.

"Hold out your hands behind you and turn around!" snapped Gramont. "No talk!"

Hearne sputtered an oath, but as the pistol jerked at him he obeyed the command. Gramont took the strips of cloth, which he had previously prepared, and bound the man's wrists.

"These are better than handcuffs," he commented. "Too many slick individuals can get rid of bracelets—but you'll have one man's job to get rid of these! Ah! a gun in your pocket, eh? Thanks."

"What t'ell you doin'?" exclaimed the bewildered Hearne.

"Placing you under arrest," said Gramont, cheerfully.

"Here, where's your warrant? You ain't no dick——"

Gramont cut short his protests with a long cloth which effectually bound his lower jaw in place and precluded any further idea of talk.

"You climb into that car, Hearne," he ordered, "and I'll attend to your feet next. That's the boy! Nothing like taking it calmly, Hearne. You didn't know that I was the fellow who pinched old Ben, did you? But I am. And before night your whole crowd will be hooked up, from the big boss down to you."

Gramont tied Dick Hearne securely, hand and foot, and then lashed him to one of the top supports of the car. When he had finished, Hearne was reasonably safe. He then climbed under the wheel again and proceeded on his way. Hearne's lashings were inconspicuous to any one whom the car passed.

It was a little after eight in the morning when Gramont drove into Paradis. He noticed that two large automobiles were standing in front of the postoffice, and that about them were a group of men who eyed him and his car with some interest. Paying no attention to these, he drove on through town without a halt.

Sweeping out along the north road, he encountered no one. When at length he reached the Ledanois farm he drove in toward the deserted house and parked the car among some trees, where it could not be seen from the road.

"You'll have some pleasant company before long, Dicky, my lad," he observed, cheerfully. A last inspection showed that his prisoner was quite secure. "In the meantime, sit and meditate upon your sins, which I trust have been many and deep. Chacherre is up for murder, and he's trying to save his neck by blowing on the remainder of your gang. We may give you a chance to do the same thing and corroborate his testimony. It's worth thinking over, isn't it?

"Perhaps you imagine that you're safe from conviction. If so, take comfort while you can—I'll chance that end of it! When Memphis Izzy comes along, I'll have a nice comfortable little conversation with him. Then we'll all join up and go back to the city together. You get the idea? Well, be good!"

Leaving the car Gramont took his way toward the bank of the bayou and followed this in the direction of the adjoining property. He looked at the water, a bitter smile upon his lips, and again made out the faint iridescent sheen of oil. When he came to the rivulet which gave birth to the oil he paused. He remembered the excitement that had so shaken him upon the discovery of this supposed seepage two days previously—he remembered ironically the visions it had aroused in his brain.

"Farewell, too sudden wealth!" he murmured. "Farewell, toil's end and dreams of luxury! I'm still a poor but honest workingman—but I still think that there's some real oil under this land. Well, we'll see about that later on, perhaps. Our company is by no means busted up yet!"

He passed on, wondering not a little at the deft skill of Jachin Fell in planting that oil; the men next door had done the work, of course. Gramont did not attempt to delude himself with the idea that Fell had acted selfishly. The whole affair had been handled with a clever secrecy, only in order that Fell's oil company might buy the land from Lucie, and that Fell might use the resultant boom to make her financially secure.

"He doesn't believe there's oil here," reflected Gramont, "and he's sincere in the belief. Where Lucie is concerned, I think the man's absolutely unselfish. He'd do anything for her! And yet Jachin Fell is an enemy, a deadly enemy, of society! Hm—these criminals show some queer streaks. You can't call a man like Fell wholly bad, not by a good deal; I'll almost regret sending him to the pen—if I do!"

He went on to an opening in the bushes which, over the low rail fence, gave him a clear view of the Gumberts property. There he paused, quickly drew back, and gained a point whence he could see without danger of his presence being discovered. He settled into immobility and watched.

That Memphis Izzy himself had not yet arrived, he was fairly certain. Near the barn were drawn up two flivvers, and sitting in chairs on the cottage veranda were three men who must have come in these cars. Gramont had come provided with binoculars, and got these out. He was not long in discovering that all three men on the veranda were strangers to him. They, no doubt, were men in the lottery game, waiting for Gumberts to arrive. Gramont turned his attention to the other buildings.

Both the barn and shop were open, and the buzzing thrum of machinery bore witness that the mechanics were hard at work upon the stolen cars. Gramont thought of Ben Chacherre, still tied and lashed to the chair in his room, and wondered what was to be found under the rear seat of Ben's car. He could see the car from where he lay.

The minutes dragged interminably, and Gramont settled down to a comfortable position in the grass. Would Fell come? He hoped so, but strongly doubted it. Fell appeared to be merely "the boss" and it was Gumberts who was actually managing the lottery swindle.

Nine o'clock came and passed. A third flivver came roaring into the opening, and Gramont leaned forward intently. Three workers came to the door of the shop. A single man left the flivver and greeted them, then went on to the cottage and joined the other three on the veranda. He was greeted with no excitement. The house door remained closed. The newcomer lighted a cigarette and sat on the steps.

"Evidently he's not Gumberts," thought Gramont. "Seven of them so far, eh? This is going to be a real job and no mistake."

Almost on his thought, a high-powered and noiseless car came sweeping down the road and he knew at once that Memphis Izzy had arrived. He knew it intuitively, even before he obtained a good glimpse of the broad, heavy figure, and the dominating features. Memphis Izzy was far from handsome, but he possessed character.

"Where's the Goog?" As he left the car, which he had driven himself, Gumberts lifted his voice in a bull-like roar that carried clearly to Gramont. "Where's Charlie the Goog?"

The mechanics appeared hurriedly. One of them, no other than Gramont's friend of the adenoidal aspect, who seemed to own the mellifluous title of Charlie the Goog, hastened to the side of Gumberts, and the latter gave him evident directions regarding some repair to the car. Then, turning, Memphis Izzy strode to the cottage. He nodded greetings to the four men who awaited him, took a bunch of keys from his pocket, and opened the cottage door. All five vanished within.

Gramont rose. A moment previously, fever had thrilled him; the excitement of the manhunt had held him trembling. Now he was cool again, his fingers touching the pistol in his pocket, his eyes steady. He glanced at his watch, and nodded.

"It's time!" he murmured. "Let's hope there'll be no slip-up! All ready, Memphis Izzy? So am I. Let's go!"

Unhurried and openly, he advanced, making his leisurely way toward the barn and shop. Charlie the Goog, who was bent over the car of Gumberts, was first to discern his approach, and straightened up. Gramont waved his hand in greeting. Charlie the Goog turned his head and called his brethren, who came into sight, staring at Gramont.

The latter realized that if he passed them the game was won. If they stopped him, he bade fair to lose everything.

"Hello, boys!" he called, cheerily, as he drew near. "I came out on an errand for the boss—got a message for Gumberts. Where is he? In the house?"

The others nodded, plainly mistrusting him yet puzzled by his careless manner and his reference to Fell.

"Sure," answered Charlie the Goog. "Go right in—he's in the big front room."

"Thanks."

Gramont continued his way, conscious that they were staring after him. If there was anything phony about him, they evidently considered that Memphis Izzy would take care of the matter very ably.

The steps of the cottage porch creaked protestingly as Gramont ascended them. Perhaps Memphis Izzy recognized an unaccustomed footstep; perhaps that conversation outside had penetrated to him. Gramont entered the front door into the hall, and as he did so, Gumberts opened the door on his right and stood gazing at him—rather, glaring.

"Who're you?" he demanded, roughly.

"Came out with a message from Mr. Fell," responded Gramont at once. "Brought some orders, I should say——"

The sixth sense of Memphis Izzy, which had carried him uncaught into a grizzled age, must have flashed a warning to his crook's brain. In the man's eyes Gramont read a surge of suspicion, and knew that his bluff could be worked no longer.

"Here's his note," he said, and reached into his pocket.

Gumberts' hand flashed down, but halted as Gramont's pistol covered him.

"Back into that room, and do it quickly," said Gramont, stepping forward. "Quick!"

Memphis Izzy obeyed. Gramont stood in the doorway, his eyes sweeping the room and the men inside. Startled, all four of them had risen and were staring at him. In his other hand he produced the automatic which he had taken from Dick Hearne.

"The first word from any of you gentlemen," he declared, "will draw a shot. I'm doing all the talking here. Savvy?"

They stood staring, paralyzed by this apparition. They had been sitting about a table which was heaped with papers and with packages of money. A large safe in the wall stood open. Beside the table was a small mail sack, partially emptied of its contents; torn envelopes littered the floor.

That this was the headquarters of at least a section of the lottery gang Gramont saw without need of explanation.

"You're under arrest," said Gramont, quietly. "The game's up, Gumberts. Hands up, all of you! Dick Hearne has peached on the whole gang, and from the boss down you're all in for a term in stir. You with the derby! Take Gumberts' gun, and those of your companions, then your own; throw 'em on the floor in the corner, and if you make the wrong kind of a move, heaven help you! Step lively, there!"

One of the men who wore a derby on the back of his head obeyed the command. All five of the men facing Gramont realized that a single shout would call help from outside, but in the eyes of Gramont they read a strict attention to business. It was altogether too probable that one man who dared arrest them alone would shoot to kill at the first false move—and not even Memphis Izzy himself opened his mouth.

Each man there had a revolver or pistol, and one by one the weapons clattered into the corner. Gumberts stood motionless, licking his thick lips, unuttered curses in his glaring eyes. And in that instant Gramont heard the porch steps creak, and caught a low, startled cry.

"Hey, boss! They's a gang comin' on the run——"

It was Charlie the Goog, bursting in upon them in wild haste. Gramont stepped into the room and turned slightly, covering with one of his weapons the intruder, who stood aghast in the doorway as he comprehended the scene.

No words passed. Staring at the five men, then at Gramont, the adenoidal mechanic gulped once—and like a flash acted. He ducked low, and fired from his pocket. Gramont fired at the same instant, and the heavy bullet, catching Charlie the Goog squarely in the chest, hurled his body half across the room.

With the shots Memphis Izzy flung himself forward in a headlong rush. That desperate shot of the little mechanic had broken Gramont's right arm above the wrist; before he could fire a second time, with the weapon in his left hand, Gumberts had wrested the pistol aside and was struggling with him. The other four came into the melee full weight.

Gramont went down under a crashing blow. Over him leaped Memphis Izzy and rushed into the doorway—then stopped with astounding abruptness and lifted his arms. After him the other four followed suit. Two men, panting a little, stood outside the door and covered them with shotguns.

"Back up," they ordered, curtly. Memphis Izzy and his four friends obeyed.

"Tie 'em, boys," said Gramont, rising dizzily to his feet. "No, I'm not hurt—my arm's broken, I think, but let that wait. Got the ones outside?"

A stamping of feet filled the hall, and other men appeared there.

"Got two of 'em, Gramont!" responded the leader. "The third slipped in here—ah, there he is!"

Poor Charlie the Goog lay dead on the floor—a touch of heroic tragedy in his last desperate action; the one great action of his life, possibly. He had realized that it meant doom yet he had done what he could.

"I think that's all," said Gramont. "We've sure made a killing, boys—and it's a good thing you jumped in to the minute! A second later and they'd have done for me. Take care of that evidence, will you? Get that mail sack and the letters particularly; if they've been working their lottery outside the state, it'll be a Federal matter."

Gumberts, who was being tied up with his friends, uttered a hoarse cry.

"Who are you guys? You can't do this without authority——"

"Don't be silly, Memphis Izzy!" said Gramont, smiling a little, then twitching to the pain of his arm. "These friends of mine are members with me of the American Legion, and they've come along at my request to put you crooks where you belong. As for authority, you can ask and go hang.

"Here, boys, I've got to get out to that barn. Come along, some of you! We'll get my arm tied up later. Nobody hurt out here?"

"Not a scrap, even," responded the leader, with a trace of disgust. "All three of those bums were outside, and we covered 'em as we came out of the brush. The one that got away did so by getting his friends between us and him. But you attended to him."

"And he attended to me likewise," added Gramont, not without a wince of pain.

He led the way out to the barn, and, the others trooping in behind him, entered. He pointed out the car which had brought Chacherre here previously, and ordered the extra seat in back opened up.

"I think there's a bundle inside," he said. "What's in it, I don't know——"

"Here we are, cap."

A bundle was produced, and opened. In it was found the aviator's costume which Gramont had worn as the Midnight Masquer, and which Chacherre had stolen with the loot. Wrapped among the leathern garments was an automatic pistol.

Gramont stood aghast before this discovery, as realization of what it meant broke full upon him.

"Good lord!" he exclaimed, amazedly. "Boys—why, it must have been Ben Chacherre who killed Maillard! See if that pistol has been used——"

The Midnight Masquer had fired two bullets into Maillard. Two cartridges were gone from this automatic.

Chapter 15: When the Heavens Fall

The chief of police entered the office of Jachin Fell, high in the Maison Blanche building, at eight o'clock on Friday evening. Mr. Fell glanced up at him in surprise.

"Hello, chief! What's up?"

The officer gazed at him in some astonishment.

"What's up? Why, I came around to see you, of course!"

Jachin Fell smiled whimsically. "To see me? Well, chief, that's good of you; sit down and have a cigar, eh? What's the matter? You look rather taken aback."

"I am," said the other, bluntly. "Didn't you expect me?"

"No," said Jachin Fell, halting suddenly in the act of reaching for a cigar and turning his keen gaze upon the chief. "Expect you? No!"

"It's darned queer, then! That chap Gramont called me up about ten minutes ago and said to get around here as quick as I could make it, that you wanted to see me."

"Gramont!" Jachin Fell frowned. "Where's Ben Chacherre? Haven't you found him yet?"

"Nary a sign of him, chief."

The door opened, and Henry Gramont appeared, his right hand bandaged and in a sling.

"Good evening, gentlemen!" he said, smiling.

"Here's Gramont now," exclaimed Fell. "Did you call the chief over here——"

"I sure did," and Gramont came forward. "I wanted to see you two gentlemen together, and so arranged it. Miss Ledanois is to be here at nine, Fell?"

The little man nodded, his eyes intent upon Gramont. He noticed the bandaged arm.

"Yes. Have you been hurt?"

"Slightly." Gramont brought up a chair across the desk from Fell, and sat down. He put his left hand in his breast pocket, and brought forth a document which he handed to the chief of police. "Cast your eye over that, chief, and say nothing. You're here to listen for the present. Here's something to cover your case, Mr. Fell."

Gramont produced his automatic from the pocket of his coat, and laid it on the desk before him. There was a moment of startled silence. The officer, looking over the paper which Gramont had handed him, seemed to find it of sudden, intense interest.

"What means all this mystery and melodramatic action, Gramont?" demanded Jachin Fell, a slight sneer in his eyes, his voice quite toneless.

"It means," said Gramont, regarding him steadily, "that you're under arrest. I went out to the Gumberts place on Bayou Terrebonne this morning, arrested Memphis Izzy Gumberts and four other men engaged in operating a lottery, and also arrested two mechanics who were engaged in working on stolen cars. We took in, further, a gentleman by the name of Dick Hearne; a lesser member of the gang, who is now engaged in dictating a confession. Just a moment, chief! I prefer to do the talking at present."

The chief of police had been about to interfere. At this, however, he leaned back in his chair, tapping in his hand the paper which he had perused. He looked very much as though in danger from a stroke of apoplexy.

Gramont smiled into the steady, unfaltering eyes of Fell.

"You are next on the programme," he said, evenly. "We know that you are at the head of an organized gang, which is not only operating a lottery through this and adjacent states, but also is conducting an immense business in stolen automobiles. Therefore——"

"Just one minute, please," said Jachin Fell. "Do you forget, Mr. Gramont, the affair of the Midnight Masquer? You are a very zealous citizen, I have no doubt, but——"

"I was about to add," struck in Gramont, "that your pleasant friend Ben Chacherre is charged with the murder of the sheriff of Terrebonne Parish, in which I have clear evidence against him, having been present at the scene of the crime. He is also charged with the murder of Joseph Maillard——-"

"What!" From both Fell and the officer broke an exclamation of undisguised amazement.

"Quite true, I assure you," said Gramont. "The evidence is, at least, a good deal clearer than the evidence against young Maillard."

"My heavens!" said Fell, staring. "I never dreamed that Chacherre——"

"Perhaps you didn't." Gramont shrugged his shoulders. "Neither did any one else. I imagine that Ben learned of this room and drinking party, and rightly decided that he could make a rich haul off a small crowd of drunken young sports. He had the costume stolen from my car, as you know, also the automatic which went with it. Two shots were missing from the automatic when we found it in Ben's possession; and you remember the Masquer fired twice at the time Maillard was killed."

"Ah! I always said young Maillard wasn't guilty!" exclaimed the chief.

"And your man Hammond——" began Fell. Gramont interposed.

"You thought you had Hammond sewed up tight, didn't you? To use the language of your favourite game, Fell, development is everything, and the player who gives up a pawn for the sake of development shows that he is possessed of the *idee grande*. You took the pawn, or thought you did—but I've taken the game!

"In one way, Fell, I'm very sorry to arrest you. It's going to hurt a mutual friend of ours. I realize that you've been trying very hard to be unselfish toward her, and I think that you've been perfectly sincere in this respect. Nonetheless, I've only one duty in the matter, and I propose to carry it through to the finish."

Fell's keen eyes sparkled angrily.

"You're a very zealous citizen, young man," he said, softly. "I see that you've been hurt. I trust your little game did not result in casualties?"

Gramont nodded. "Charlie the Goog went west. He was desperate, I fancy; at all events he got me in the arm, and I had to shoot him. Memphis Izzy hardly justified his tremendous reputation, for he yielded like a lamb."

"So you killed the Goog, eh?" said Fell. "Very zealous, Mr. Gramont! And I suppose that the exigencies of the case justified you, a private citizen, in carrying arms and using them? Who aided you in this marvellous affair?"

"A number of friends from my post of the American Legion," said Gramont, evenly.

"Ah! This organization is going in for politics, then?"

"Not for politics, Fell; for justice. I deputized them to assist me."

"Deputized!" repeated Fell, slowly.

"Certainly." Gramont smiled. "You see, this lottery business has been going on for a year or more. Some time ago, before I came to New Orleans, the governor of this state appointed me a special officer to investigate the matter. There is my commission, which the chief has been reading. It gives me a good deal of power, Fell; quite enough power to gather in you and your bunch.

"I might add that I have secured an abundance of evidence to prove that the lottery gang, under your supervision, has extended its operations to adjacent states. This, as you are aware, brings the affair into Federal hands if necessary."

The chief of police looked very uneasily from Gramont to Jachin Fell, and back again. Fell sat erect in his chair, staring at Gramont.

"You were the original Midnight Masquer," said Fell in his toneless voice. At this direct charge, and at Gramont's assent, the chief started in surprise.

"Yes. One reason was that I suspected someone in society, someone high up in New Orleans, to be connected with the gang; but I never dreamed that you were the man, Fell. I rather suspected young Maillard. I am now glad to say that I was entirely wrong. You were the big boss, Fell, and you're going to serve time for it."

Fell glanced at the chief, who cleared his throat as if about to speak. At this moment, however, a sharp knock sounded at the door.

"Come!" called Gramont.

A man entered. It was one of Gramont's deputies, who happened also to be a reporter from one of the morning papers of the city. He carried several sheets of paper which he laid before Gramont. He glanced at Fell, who recognized him and exchanged a nod of greeting, then returned his attention to Gramont.

"Ah!" said the latter with satisfaction, as he examined the papers. "So Hearne has given up everything, has he? Does this confession implicate Mr. Fell, here?"

"Well, rather," drawled the other, cheerfully. "And see here, cap! There are two more of us in the crowd and we've arranged to split the story. We'd like to rush the stuff to our papers the minute you give the word, because——"

"I know." Gramont returned the papers that bore the confession of Hearne. "You've made copies of this, of course? All right. Shoot the stuff in to your papers right away, if you wish."

Fell raised a hand to check the other.

"One moment, please!" he said, his eyes boring into the newspaper man. "Will you also take a message from me to the editor of your newspaper—and see that it goes to the others as well?"

"If Mr. Gramont permits, yes."

"Go ahead," said Gramont, wondering what Fell would try now. He soon learned.

"Then," pursued Fell, evenly, "you will kindly inform the editors of your papers that, in case my name appears in connection with this matter, I shall immediately institute suit for libel. No matter what Mr. Gramont may say or do, I assure you fully that no publicity is going to attach to me in this matter. Neither, I may add, am I going to be arrested. That is all, sir."

Gramont smiled. "Take the message if you see fit, by all means," he said, carelessly. "You may also take my fullest assurance that within twenty minutes you will observe Mr. Fell safely in jail. That's all."

The newspaper man saluted and departed, grinning.

Gramont leaned forward, the harsh lines of his face spelling determination as he looked at Jachin Fell.

"So you won't be arrested, eh? Let's see. I know that this gang of yours has influence running up into high places, and that this influence has power. The governor knows it also. That is why I was appointed to investigate this lottery game secretly, and in my own way. That is why, also, I brought the chief of police here to-night."

He turned to the perturbed officer, and spoke coldly.

"Now, chief, you've seen my authority, you've heard my charges, and you know they will be proved up to the hilt. Dick Hearne gave up the names of most of the lottery gang and their confederates; my deputies already wired to their various places of operation for the purpose of securing their arrest. We'll make a clean sweep.

"The same may be said of the automobile gang, although we will probably miss a few of the smaller fry. What other forms of criminality the organization may be engaged in I can't say at this moment; but we have secured quite enough evidence. Are you willing to arrest Jachin Fell, or not?"

The chief cleared his throat.

"Why, Mr. Gramont," he observed, nervously, "about the rest of the gang, we'll take care of 'em, sure! But it's different with Mr. Fell here. He's a friend of the senator——"

"Different, hell!" snapped Gramont, angrily. "He's a criminal, no matter who his friends may be, and I have the proof of it!"

"Well, that may be so," admitted the chief of police. "But this thing is goin' to raise one hell of a scandal, all up and down the state! You know that as well as I do. Now, if I was you, I'd act kind of slow——"

Gramont smiled bitterly.

"Perhaps you would, chief. In fact, I don't doubt that you would. But you are not *me*. Now, as a duly-appointed officer acting under authority of the governor of the state, I call upon you to arrest this criminal, and I make you duly responsible for his safe-keeping. Do you dare refuse?"

The chief hesitated. He looked at Fell for help, but none came. Fell seemed to be rather amused by the situation.

"Well," said the chief, "I ain't seen the evidence yet——"

"I'll show you some evidence of another kind, chief," said Gramont, sternly quiet. "Outside the door, here, there are two men who will obey my orders and my authority. If you dare refuse to do your duty you will yourself be taken from this room under arrest, on a John Doe warrant which is already prepared and waiting; and you will be charged with being an accomplice of this gang. Now choose, and choose quickly!"

Gramont leaned back in his chair. The purpling features of the chief were streaming with perspiration; the man was in a frightful dilemma, and his plight was pitiable. At this instant Jachin Fell interposed.

"Let me speak, please," he said, gently. "My dear Mr. Gramont, it has just occurred to me that there may be a compromise——"

"I'm not compromising," snapped Gramont.

"Certainly not; I speak of our mutual friend here," and Fell indicated the chief with a bland gesture. "I believe that Judge Forester of this city is at present consulting with the governor at Baton Rouge on political matters. With them, also, is Senator Flaxman, who has come from Washington on the same errand. Now, it would be a very simple matter to end all this anxiety. Suppose that you call up the governor on long distance, from this telephone, and get his assurance that I am not to be arrested. Then you'll be convinced."

Gramont laughed with deep anger.

"You gangsters are all alike!" he said, turning to the desk telephone. "You think that because you have planted your slimy tentacles in high places you can do anything with absolute impunity. But the governor of this state is not in your clutches.

"He's a man, by heaven! I have his assurance that he'll prosecute to the limit whoever is behind this criminal gang—and he keeps his word! Don't think that if your friend the senator is with him, you will be saved. I'll call him, if only to show the chief, here, that influence is not going to count in this game."

Gramont took down the receiver, called long distance, and put in a hurried call for the executive mansion, asking for the governor in person.

"So you think that he's immune from influence, do you?" Jachin Fell smiled patronizingly and lighted a fresh cigar. The chief of police was mopping his brow.

"My dear Gramont, you exhibit a youthful confidence in human nature! Let me topple your clay-footed idol from its pedestal in a hurry. Mention to the governor that you have me under arrest, and that I have asked him to speak with Judge Forester and Senator Flaxman before confirming the arrest. I'll wager you five hundred dollars——"

The smile in Fell's pale eyes drove Gramont into a cold fury of rage.

"You devil! So your damnable influence goes as far as those two men, does it—those men who are respected above all others in this city? By the lord, I'll call your bluff! I know the governor, and I know he doesn't give a damn for all the dirty crooks and slimy politicians on earth!"

"What sublime faith!" laughed Fell, softly.

The telephone rang sharply. Taunted almost beyond endurance, Gramont seized the instrument and made answer. In a moment he had the governor on the wire. His gaze went exultantly to Fell.

"Governor, this is Henry Gramont speaking," he said. "I've just succeeded in my work, as I wired you this afternoon—no, hold on a minute! This is important.

"The head of the entire gang is a man here in New Orleans by the name of Jachin Fell. Yes, Fell. I find it very hard to get him arrested. Fell boasts that his influence is superior to any that I can bring to bear. He asks that you speak with Judge Forester and Senator Flaxman before confirming the arrest, and boasts that you will order me to keep hands off.

"Speak with them, governor! If they're in the gang, too, don't you worry. You confirm this arrest, and I'll put Fell behind the bars if I have to turn all New Orleans inside out. Go ahead! I know that you can't be reached by any of these crooks—I'm merely calling Fell's bluff. We have the chief of police here, and he's sweating. Eh? Sure. Take as long as you like, governor."

He smiled grimly at Jachin Fell as he waited. Two minutes passed—three—four. Then he heard the voice of the governor again.

"Yes?"

"Don't arrest him, Gramont."

"What?" Gramont gasped.

"Don't touch him, I said! Get in all the others, no matter who they are, but leave Fell alone——"

"You damned coward!" shouted Gramont, in a heat of fury. "So this is the way you keep your promises, is it? And I thought you were above all influences—real American! You're a hell of a governor—oh, I don't want to hear any more from you."

He jerked up the receiver.

There was a moment of dead silence in the room. The chief mopped his brow, in evident relief. Jachin Fell sat back in his chair and scrutinized Gramont with his thin-lipped smile.

Gramont sat helpless, wrung by chagrin, rage, and impotency. There was nothing he could say, nothing he could do. The man behind him had failed him. The entire power of the state, which had been behind him, had failed him. There was no higher power to which he could appeal, except the power of the Federal Government. His head jerked up sharply.

"Fell, I've got the evidence on you, and I've got the evidence to put this lottery business into Federal hands. Boys! Come in here!"

At his shout the door opened and two of his men entered. Gramont looked at the chief.

"You're willing to take care of all the rest of the gang, chief?"

"Sure," assented the officer, promptly.

"All right. Boys, turn over the whole crowd to the chief, and I'll trust you to see that they're properly booked and jailed. Turn over all the evidence likewise, except that mail sack. Have that brought up here, to this room, and see that the corridor outside is kept guarded. Get me?"

The two saluted. "Yes, sir."

"Good. Send to the Federal building, find out where there's an agent of the Department of Justice, and get him here. Have him here inside of fifteen minutes."

Fell smiled. "I can save you time, gentlemen. The agent in charge of this district will probably be home at this hour. I can give you his address——"

He did so. In the pale eyes Gramont read an imperturbable challenge. The effrontery of the man appalled him. He turned to his men.

"Confirm fully that he *is* the agent before you get him," he ordered, curtly. "Have him bring one of his deputy agents likewise, to meet you here. That's all, chief, if you'll go along with these men, you'll be put in charge of our prisoners and evidence. I've left a guard at the

Gumberts place at Terrebonne, and I'd suggest that you go through the residence of Gumberts here in town. You might find evidence. That's all."

The chief departed without a word. It was obvious that he was mighty glad to be gone. Gramont and Fell were left alone together.

"My dear Gramont, your devotion to duty is Roman in spirit," said Jachin Fell, lightly. "I really regret that circumstances so conspire to defeat you! Why can't you be satisfied with bagging so many other victims? You can't bag me——"

"Can't I?" said Gramont, taking a cigar and biting at it. He was cooler now. "By heavens, Fell, there's one thing in this country that you and no other man can reach with any influence, political bribery, or crooked connections— and that's the Government of the United States! You can reach judges and senators and governors, but you can't reach the unknown and humble men who carry the badge of the Department of Justice!"

Fell made a slight gesture.

"Human nature, my dear Gramont. It is quite true that I have not established this gang of criminals, as you call them, without taking proper precautions. Memphis Izzy, for instance, has influence that reaches far and wide. So have I. So have others in the party. I give you my assurance that your Department of Justice man will not arrest me."

Gramont paled.

"If——" He choked on the word, then touched the automatic on the desk before him. "If he won't, Jachin Fell, I'll put a bullet through you myself!"

For the first time the pale eyes of Jachin Fell looked slightly troubled.

"You'll hang if you do," he said, gently.

"I'll be damned if I don't!" snapped Gramont, and put the weapon in his lap.

Chapter 16: The Impregnability of Mr. Fell

Jachin Fell glanced at his watch.

"Lucie will be here at any minute now," he observed. "I suppose your sense of duty will force you to disclose everything to her?"

Gramont merely nodded, tight-lipped. A knock at the door, and one of his men entered with the sack of mail they had taken as evidence.

"A lady is coming here at any moment," said Gramont. "Allow her to enter."

The other saluted and departed.

"A sense of duty is a terrible thing," and Jachin Fell sighed. "What about the oil company? Are you going to let Miss Ledanois' fortunes go to wrack and ruin?"

"Better that," said Gramont, "than to have her profit come through criminal money and means. She'd be the first to say so, herself. But I'll tell you this: I'm convinced that there is oil under the land of hers! If she'll agree, I'll put up what money I have against her land; we'll be able to have one well drilled at least, on the chance!"

"If it's dry," said Fell, "you'll be broke."

"I can always get work," and Gramont laughed harshly.

Fell regarded him in silence a moment. Then: "I think Lucie loves you, Gramont."

A trembling seized Gramont; a furious impulse to shoot the man down as he sat. Did he have the baseness to try and save himself through Lucie? Something of his stifled anger must have shone in his eyes, for Jachin Fell laid down his cigar and continued quickly:

"Don't misunderstand. I say that I think she cares for you; it is merely surmise on my part. Lucie is one person for whom I'd do anything. I stand and have stood in the place of a parent to her. She is very dear to me. I have a special reason for intruding on your personal affairs in this manner, and some right to ask you in regard to your intentions."

"I don't recognize any right whatever on your part," said Gramont, steadily.

Fell smiled. "Ah! Then you are in love. Well, youth must be served!"

"I'd like to know one thing," struck in Gramont. "That is, why you were so cursed anxious to get something on my man Hammond! And why you held the Midnight Masquer affair over me as a threat. Did you suspect my business?"

Fell threw back his head and laughed in a hearty amusement that was quite unrestrained.

"That," he responded, "is really humorous! Do you know, I honestly thought you a fortune-hunter from Europe? When I suspected you of being the Midnight Masquer, and afterward, I was convinced that you, and very likely Hammond as well, were very clever swindlers of some kind. There, I confess, I made a grave error. My friend Gumberts never forgets faces, and he said to me, one day, that Hammond's face was vaguely familiar to him, but he could not place the man. That led me to think——"

"Ah!" exclaimed Gramont. "Gumberts saw Hammond years ago, when he was escaping from the law—and to think he remembered! Hammond told me about it."

"That's why I wanted you and Hammond in my gang," said Fell. "I thought it would be very well to get you into the organization for my own purposes."

"Thanks," answered Gramont, drily. "I got in, didn't I?"

Without a knock the door opened and Lucie Ledanois entered.

"Good evening, stockholders!" she exclaimed. "Do you know there's a crowd down in the street—policemen and automobiles and a lot of excitement?"

"Allow me," said Gramont, taking her coat and placing a chair for her. "Oh, yes, we've had quite a strenuous evening, Miss Ledanois."

"Your hand! Why, what has happened?"

"One of Mr. Fell's friends tried to shoot me. Will you sit down, please? You remember that I warned you regarding a shock that would come; and now I must explain." Gramont gravely handed her his commission from the governor, and resumed his seat. "When I say that I have come here, not to attend a meeting of our oil company, but to arrest Mr. Fell, you will understand. I am very sorry, Lucie, to have to tell you all this, for I know your attachment to him."

"Arrest—you, Uncle Jachin?" The girl glanced from the paper to Fell, who nodded. "And you, Henry—a special officer of the governor's? Why—this isn't a joke of some kind?"

"None whatever, my dear," said Fell, quietly. "Mr. Gramont is to be congratulated. He has discovered that I was the head of a large organization of criminals. He has there, under the table, a sack of mail which proves that my organization was conducting a lottery throughout several states; we are now expecting the arrival of Federal agents, to whom Gramont intends to turn me over as a prisoner."

"Oh!" The girl stared at him, wide-eyed. Her voice broke. "It—it can't be true——"

"It is quite true, my dear," and Jachin Fell smiled. "But don't let it distress you in the least, I beg. Here, if I mistake not, are your Department of Justice friends, Gramont."

A knock at the door, and it opened to admit one of Gramont's men.

"Here they are, sir—the chief agent and a deputy. Shall I let them in?"

Gramont nodded. Two men entered the room, and Gramont dismissed his own man with a gesture. He saw that the agents both nodded to Fell.

"Do you gentlemen know this man?" he demanded, rising.

"Yes," said one of them, regarding him keenly. "Who sent for us?"

"I did." Gramont gave his name, and handed them his commission. "I have been investigating a lottery which has been conducted in this state for a long time by an organization of very clever criminals. Jachin Fell is the man at the head of this organization. To-day I rounded up the entire gang, and procured all the evidence necessary. Under that table is a sack of mail proving that the lottery has been extended to other states, and that part of its operations have been conducted by means of the United States mails.

"The lesser members of the gang are in custody. The police department will not arrest this man Fell; his influence and that of his gang is extensive in political fields and elsewhere. I have called up the governor, and have been told not to arrest him. I have disregarded these facts, and I now call upon you to hold him in custody as a Federal prisoner. He has boasted to me that you will not touch him—and if you don't, there's going to be a shakeup that will make history! Now go to it."

The chief agent laid Gramont's commission on the table and looked at Jachin Fell. For an instant there was a dead silence. Then, when the Federal man spoke, Gramont was paralyzed.

"I'm very sorry, Mr. Gramont, to have to refuse——"

"What!" cried Gramont, incredulously. "Do you dare stand there and——"

"One moment please," said Fell, his quiet voice breaking in. "It is quite true that I have organized all the criminals possible, Mr. Gramont, and have put the underground lottery into a systematized form. I have done this by the authority of the United States, in order to apprehend Memphis Izzy Gumberts and other men at one crack. These gentlemen will tell you that I am a special agent of the Department of Justice, employed in that capacity through the efforts of Judge Forester and Senator Flaxman. I regret that this had to be held so secret that not even the governor himself was aware of it until this evening. The conflict was quite unavoidable. Not a member of that gang must become aware of my real identity."

Fell turned to the two agents, who were smiling.

"I would suggest that you take this sack of mail, and arrange with the chief of police in regard to the prisoners," he said. "The chief, of course, must suspect nothing."

Gramont sank into his chair, the automatic dropping from his hand. He was suddenly dazed, thunderstruck. Yet he had to believe. He was dimly aware that Lucie had gone to Jachin Fell, her arms about his neck. He stared from unseeing eyes.

Realization smote him like a blow, numbing his brain. He saw now why the governor had conferred with Judge Forester and the senator, why he had been ordered off the trail. He saw now why Fell had preserved secrecy so great that even to the chief of police his impregnable position was supposedly due to influence higher up.

He saw how Fell must have been working month after month, silently and terribly, to form one compact organization of the most talented criminals within reach—headed by Memphis Izzy, the man who had laughed at the government for years! And he saw himself, furious, raging like a madman——

Gramont dropped his head into his hands. The pain of his forgotten wounded arm stabbed him like a knife. He jerked his head sharply up, and was aware that the agents had departed. He was alone with Lucie and Fell, and the latter was rising and holding out his hand, smiling.

"Gramont, you got ahead of me in this deal, and I congratulate you with all my heart!" said Fell, earnestly. "Neither of us suspected the part played by the other man; but you've done the work and done it well. Will you shake hands?"

Gramont confusedly took the hand extended to him.

"I've been a fool," he said, slowly. "I might have guessed that something unusual was——"

"No; how could you guess?" said Fell. "There are three men in Baton Rouge who know the truth, and three persons in this room. That's all, outside of the regular government men. I had not told even Lucie, here! I dared not. And I dare say nothing even now. To the underworld at large I will be known as the crook whom not even the government could touch; in days to come I may be of untold service to my country."

"I'm so glad!" Lucie took Gramont's hand as Jachin Fell dropped it, and Gramont looked down to meet her brimming eyes. "For a moment I thought that all the world had gone mad—but now——"

Jachin Fell regarded them for an instant, then he quietly went to the door.

"If you will excuse me one moment," he said, "I shall speak with your men who are on guard, Gramont. I—ah—I will be back in a moment, as Eliza said when she crossed the ice; and we may then discuss business. If you agree, I think that your company may proceed upon the original lines, and we shall set to work drilling for oil without delay——"

Gramont scarcely heard the words, nor did he hear the door close. He was still looking into the eyes of Lucie Ledanois, and wondering if the message they held were really meant for him.

Chapter 17: Mi-Careme

A nameless gentleman from the effete North was enjoying for the first time the privileges of a guest card at the Chess and Checkers. In a somewhat perplexed manner he approached the secretary's desk and obtained a cigar. Then he paused, listening to the sounds of revelry which filled the club, and which came roaring in from the city streets outside.

"Say!" he addressed the secretary. "What's this Mi-Careme I've been reading about in the papers, anyhow? I thought everything was tight as a clam down here after Mardi Gras! It's still the Lenten season, isn't it? Mardi Gras doesn't come more than once a year? Then what's all the celebration about?"

The secretary smiled.

"Certainly, sir, it's still Lent. But the French people have what they call Mi-Careme, or Mid-Lent, and they certainly give it a big celebration! You see, it's a night halfway through Lent, when they can enjoy themselves to the limit—let off steam, as it were. We're having several dinner parties here in the club to-night, for the occasion."

A slightly built little man, who had much the air of a shy clerk—had it not been for his evening attire—approached the desk. He signed a check for a handful of cigars, which he stowed away.

"Please provide a fresh box of the El Reys later," he said to the secretary. "Most of my party is here, I believe."

"I'll send them up, Mr. Fell," answered the secretary, quickly. "Yes, I think the dining room is all ready for you, sir. By the way, Mr. Gramont was looking for you a moment ago—ah! Here he comes now!"

Jachin Fell turned. Gramont was plunging at him, a yellow telegraph form in his hand, excitement in his eyes.

"Look here, Jachin! This wire just came in from Hammond—you know, I left him in charge of things down at Bayou Terrebonne! Read it, man—read it! They've struck oil-sands at five hundred feet—and sands at five hundred, with these indications, mean a gusher at a thousand! Where's Lucie? Have you brought her?"

"She's upstairs. Well, well!" Jachin Fell glanced at the telegram, and returned it. "So oil is actually found! This is certainly going to be one big night, as Eliza said when she crossed the ice! Come along. Let's find Lucie and tell her about it——"

The two men turned away together.

After them gazed the man from the North, not a little agape over what he had chanced to hear. Before the wondering questions in his eyes the assiduous secretary made haste to enlighten him.

"That's Mr. Gramont, sir. They say that he used to be a real prince, over in France, and that he threw it up because he wanted to be an American. Mr. Fell is having a dinner upstairs—it's Mr. Gramont's engagement, you know—and the Mi-Careme ball afterward——"

"Oh, I know, I know," and the man from the North sighed a little. "I was reading all about that in the paper. Fell is one of the crack chess players here, isn't he?"

The secretary smiled.

"Well, he plays a very fair game, sir—a very fair game indeed!"

THE END

Resurrected Press Mysteries From Louis Tracy

The Albert Gate Mystery
Four men murdered and a fortune in diamonds belonging to the Turkish Sultan stolen, while the Foreign Office official in charge has gone missing. Was it a common jewelry theft or was it a case of international intrigue? This is the question that barrister detective Reginald Brett must solve.

The Bartlett Mystery
When Ronald Tower is murdered on his way to a bridge game on the yacht Sans Souci it at first appears a common crime. But as Rex Carshaw finds, a tragic case of mistaken identity leads to political scandal among the rich and powerful of New York.

The Strange Case of Mortimer Fenley
When the wealthy Mortimer Fenley is struck down by a shot from an express rifle on the steps of his mansion, detectives Winter and Furneaux of Scotland Yard must find the culprit. Was it the artist who claimed he was painting a picture at the time of the shot? The disaffected younger son? Or is there another suspect?

The Stowmarket Mystery
For five generations the Fergus-Hume family has been cursed. Each of the baronets has met a violent end. When the fifth baronet is found slain by a ceremonial Japanese dagger, suspicion falls on his cousin David. It falls to barrister detective Reginald Brett to prove his innocence and find the real murder in a case that spans two continents and as many centuries.

Resurrected Press Mysteries by J. S. Fletcher

The Orange-Yellow Diamond
When an elderly pawnbroker is murdered in the London parish of Paddington, a young, down on his luck writer is accused of the crime. But then it's found the pawnbroker had had in his possession an extraordinary South African diamond worth over eighty-thousand pounds —a diamond that's now missing. It falls to Melky Rubenstein to unravel the mystery and prove the young man's innocence.

The Middle Temple Murder
When an elderly man's body is found on the steps of chambers in the Midde Temple, one of the Inns of Court, it falls to newspaperman Frank Spargo and Detective-Sergeant Rathbury to solve the crime. The murdered man, for indeed it was murder, was found with no money or identification on his person except for a piece of paper with the name and address of a young barrister. Who is the victim? Why was he killed? Who is the murderer?

Scarhaven Keep
Bassett Oliver, the famed actor, has gone missing. When Oliver fails to show for a rehearsal, aspiring playwright Richard Copplestone finds himself sent to the small village of Scarhaven on the northern coast of England to track down the actors movements. What he finds is mystery. Find the answers as Copplestone unravels the mystery of Scarhaven Keep.

Visit www.resurrectedpress.com

Resurrected Press Mysteries by Fergus Hume

The Green Mummy
Professor Braddock hoped to compare the burial practices of the Egyptians with those of the ancient Peruvians with his latest acquisition, the mummy of the last Inca, Caxas. But on arrival, the packing case proved to hold not the mummy, but the body of his assistant Sidney Bolton. It falls to Archie Hope to discover the murderer if he is to marry the professors step-daughter, Lucy Kendal. Who killed Bolton and where is the mummy? Was it the sea captain Hervey? The mysterious Don Pedro? Cockatoo the Polynesian servant? The professor, himself? And what has become of the emeralds? These are the questions that Hope must answer amongst the secrets of the past in The Green Mummy.

The Mystery of a Hansom Cab
"Truth is said to be stranger than fiction, and certainly the extraordinary murder which took place in Melbourne Friday morning goes a long way towards verifying that saying." Thus opens The Mystery of a Hansom Cab, the best selling mystery of the nineteenth century. When a man is found dead in a hansom cab one of Melbourne's leading citizens is accused of the murder. He pleads his innocence, yet refuses to give an alibi. It falls to a determined lawyer and an intrepid detective to find the truth, revealing long kept secrets along the way. Fergus Hume's first and perhaps most famous mystery... The Mystery Of A Hansom Cab.

Visit www.resurrectedpress.com

Resurrected Press Mysteries from the Dr. John Thorndyke Series

Dr. John Thorndyke Lecturer on Medical Jurisprudence and Forensic Medicine. Before Bones, before CSI, before Quincy, M.E– there was Dr. John Thorndyke solving the most baffling cases of Edwardian London using the latest tools of medical science. Read about his cases in:

The Eye of Osiris
John Bellingham, noted Egyptologist has vanished not once but twice in the same day. Now Dr, Thorndyke must unravel the tangled claims on his estate, solve the riddle of the missing man and find the "Eye of Osiris".

The Mystery of 31 New Inn
When Dr. Jervis is whisked away in a coach with no windows to an unknown location to treat a man in a coma from undivulged causes it is Dr. Thorndyke who must come up with the solution.

The Red Thumb Mark
The first of Dr. Thorndyke's cases finds him trying to prove the innocence of a young man accused of being a diamond thief despite the fact that his finger print was found at the scene of the crime.

John Thorndyke's Cases
More cases of medical mysteries as told by his trusted assistant Jervis, M.D. Eight stories of crime and deduction in Edwardian London.

Visit www.resurrectedpress.com

Resurrected Press Mysteries by John R. Watson & Arthur J. Rees

The Hampstead Mystery
High Court Justice Sir Horace Fewbanks found shot dead in his Hampstead home, a butler with a criminal past, a scorned lover and a hint of scandal. These are the elements of the Hampstead Mystery that Detective Inspector Chippenfield of Scotland Yard must unravel with the assistance of the ambitious Detective Rolfe. But will he be able to sort out the tangled threads of this case and arrest the culprit before he is upstaged by the celebrated gentleman detective Crewe. Follow the details of this amazing case at it plays out across Hampstead, London and Scotland until it reaches a stunning conclusion in the courts of the Old Bailey.

The Mystery of the Downs
When Harry Marsland was caught in a sudden down pour he sought shelter at Cliff Farm. Met at the door by a young woman clearly expecting someone else he is only too glad to get inside to wait out the storm. When they hear a noise upstairs in the deserted house they investigate only to discover the body of the farm's owner, Frank Lumsden, dead of a gunshot wound. Who then, killed Lumsden, and why? Who was the woman expecting and did she have any roll in the murder? These are the questions that private detective Crewe must answer in The Mystery of the Downs.

Visit www.resurrectedpress.com

Other Resurrected Press Mysteries

Mysteries on a Train

Before the Orient Express there was:

The Rome Express by Arthur Griffiths
A man is found dead in his first class sleeping compartment on the express from Rome to Paris. Who was his murderer? The Countess? The English General? His brother the clergy man? The maid who has disappeared? Is the French justice system up to solving the crime? Read about it in The Rome Express.

The Passenger from Calais by Arthur Griffiths
Colonel Basil Annesley finds he is the only passenger on the train from Calais to Lucerne. That is until a mysterious woman shows up at the last minute to book a compartment. Who is after her? What is her secret? Is she a criminal or a victim? Read about it in The Passenger from Calais

Visit us at www.resurrectedpress.com

About Resurrected Press

A division of Intrepid Ink, LLC, Resurrected Press is dedicated to bringing high quality, vintage books back into publication. See our entire catalogue and find out more at www.ResurrectedPress.com.

About Intrepid Ink, LLC

Intrepid Ink, LLC provides full publishing services to authors of fiction and non-fiction books, eBooks and websites. From editing to formatting, from publishing to marketing, Intrepid Ink gets your creative works into the hands of the people who want to read them. Find out more at www.IntrepidInk.com.